He looked interesting. Intelligent.

He was still staring at me, and I felt myself turning pink. I stood up and started playing with the dog's lead. When I looked at Luke again, he was smiling, like he was amused. Was it because he'd felt my embarrassment and was laughing at me? He probably had this effect on loads of girls. Or was he amused because I'd got the dogs' leads all tangled and almost tripped over Jerry? Oh, hell. Whatever, I thought. Nesta's lucky to have such a gorgeous boyfriend. I'd love to talk to him more about old houses and paintings. I glanced at him again as he kneeled on the ground by the bench and tried to untangle the leads.

"I'd love to talk to you more some day about old houses," he said as he looked at me. "Not many people are that interested."

I gulped. "Er nihi . . . ," I muttered as Izzie, Nesta, and Lucy came bouncing up the steps behind us and put an end to our conversation.

Mates, Dates, and Tempting Trouble

Cathy Hopkins

Simon Pulse

New York London Toronto Sydney

SIMON PULSE
An imprint of Simon & Schuster
Children's Publishing Division
1230 Avenue of the Americas, New York, NY 10020

Copyright © 2004 by Cathy Hopkins
Originally published in Great Britain in 2004 by
Piccadilly Press Ltd.
Published by arrangement with Piccadilly Press Ltd.
All rights reserved, including the right of reproduction in
whole or in part in any form.

SIMON PULSE and colophon are registered trademarks of
Simon & Schuster, Inc.

Designed by Debra Sfetsios
The text of this book was set in Bembo.

Manufactured in the United States of America
First Simon Pulse edition February 2005
4 6 8 10 9 7 5 3

Library of Congress Control Number 2004103795
ISBN-13: 978-0-689-87062-0
ISBN-10: 0-689-87062-0

Thanks as always to Brenda Gardner, Yasemin Uçar, and the ever fab team at Piccadilly Press. To Rosemary Bromley at Juvenelia. And to Steve Lovering for all his help, input, and for trekking round all the locations in the book with me.

Chapter 1

Wombat

"You go on in, T. J.," said Lucy, looking up at Kenwood House. "I'll walk the dogs."

I burst out laughing. Lucy's tiny, not even five foot; more like the dogs would walk her than the other way around. "Yeah, right," I said. "I can see the headlines now. 'Have you seen this girl? Blonde. Small'—"

"Petite," interrupted Lucy.

"Sorry, right, petite. 'Last sighted: Hampstead Heath being dragged off by three wild animals.'"

Izzie, Lucy, Nesta, and I were standing shivering outside the entrance to Kenwood House on Hampstead Heath on Saturday morning. We had Ben, Jerry, and Mojo with us. Ben and Jerry are the Labradors who belong to Lucy's family, and Mojo is my dog (breed, er . . . somewhat mixed, but he's very cute, black with a white patch over one eye, and he's my best friend, apart from Hannah, Lucy, Izzie, and Nesta, that is).

"Yeah," said Nesta, pushing stray dark hairs back into the woolly hat that she had pulled down over her ears. "Isn't the saying supposed to go, 'Mad dogs and English men go out in the midday *sun*?' Not the November rain. What are we doing out here anyway when we could be in the café like sensible people, hogging the radiators and drinking big mugs of hot chocolate?"

"If you're cold, you go in and have a look around with T. J.," said Izzie. "I'll stay with you, Lucy. I've been in. It's dead boring. Dark old rooms filled with paintings of people with glum, ugly faces staring down at you. They look like they've got plums in their mouths and pokers up their bums."

"I've been in too," I said. "Many times. And those boring paintings, some of them are by Rembrandt, Gainsborough, Reynolds; there's even a Turner. I think it's a fabulous old building."

Izzie looked at the white house and pulled a face. "Looks like an enormous wedding cake in my opinion. Not my style at all."

"It's neoclassical," I said.

Nesta looked at me with amazement. "God! How do you know this stuff?" she asked.

"Dunno," I said, shrugging. "Read it somewhere, I guess."

"Well, you must read a *lot*," said Nesta. "You always seem to know about everything. Brains *and* beauty. It's not fair."

"I am not beautiful."

"Yes, you are," said Lucy. "Remember when that journalist, Sam Denham, visited our school when we were in Year Nine, and he called you Lara Croft? Not many people can claim to look like Angelina Jolie. Your trouble is that you have no confidence about your looks."

"Yeah," said Nesta, "you could be one of those girls in the movies who wears specs, no makeup, and has her hair tied back and works in a science lab or something. Then she meets the hero, lets her hair down, takes off her glasses, and reveals that she's actually a total babe."

"And the hero falls in love with her saying, Oh but Miss Watts! You are *beeeooodiful*," said Izzie, laughing.

"Stop it," I said. I was getting embarrassed, though it was cool to be compared to Angelina Jolie.

"It is awesome, though," said Lucy. "As Nesta said, you do seem to know about all sorts of stuff the rest of us don't."

"Only what I find interesting. I mean, don't you think it's amazing that there are paintings by all these famous artists right on our doorstep? Like, ten minutes away from where we live. Some people pay fortunes to go to Venice, Amsterdam, Florence, and Paris to look at the great masters, and we only have to pop down the road. Don't you think that's brilliant?"

Izzie gave me a blank look. "No," she said.

"There's one called *The Guitar Player*, by Vermeer. I'd have thought you'd have loved that, Izzie, seeing as you're into music. She's got such a look of delight on her face. It's not like so many other paintings of the period where, you're right, the expressions are glum. It's like she was the first of many teenagers to get a guitar, and you see how it never changes through time. Even back then they were—"

"Whatever. So she's got her guitar? I bet she's still dead ugly. All those people in old paintings are," said Izzie with a playful squeeze of my arm. "I went in there years ago with Mum. Not an experience I care to repeat. Nah. Looking round stuffy old houses isn't my thing at all."

"I *love* looking around old places," I said. "The sense of history, imagining how it was in days gone by, who lived there, what they wore . . ."

"You're weird, T. J. Watts," said Izzie.

I pulled my best weird face (cross-eyed with a squiffy mouth). "But don't forget it's also famous as a location in the movies. You have to admit that's pretty cool."

"What movies?" asked Nesta.

"*Mansfield Park*. Some of that was filmed here and . . . and it's in *Notting Hill* as well. Remember

4

near the end when Hugh Grant goes to visit Julia Roberts' character when she's starring in a historical drama. That scene was filmed here. You can see the house in the background."

"Still a stuffy old place," said Izzie. "But whatever turns you on."

I rolled my eyes. "Oh, such philistines as friends. I don't know if I can bear it."

"Well, at least you don't have to hang out with a brainbox like we do," groaned Izzie.

"Neanderthal," I said.

"Swot box."

"Airhead."

"Clever clogs."

"Ignoramus."

"Wombat."

"Wombat?"

"Yeah," said Izzie with a wide grin. "Neoclassical wombat."

This time Lucy rolled her eyes. "For heaven's sake. I'm freezing. When you two have finished slagging each other off, do you think you could possibly make your mutually mad minds up what you're going to do?"

"And actually, if anyone's an airhead or whatever, it's me," said Nesta. "Izzie, you're as much of a bookworm as T. J. and don't pretend otherwise. I'll go inside and look with you, T. J. Part of my education program."

5

Nesta recently went through this phase when she was worried that we all thought that she was shallow. Then she started going out with a boy called Luke and got paranoid that he might think she wasn't very bright. As if. She's really clever, just not into reading much if she doesn't have to. She's the original good-time girl. Good times to her being boys and, well . . . more boys. A few weeks ago, though, she declared that she's going to learn about "everything." I wouldn't care if I had her looks. Even with her braces in she still looks fantastic and boys would fall at her feet whatever her IQ.

I looked around at my friends. Lucy's teeth were chattering. Izzie had a red nose from the cold, her dark hair was hanging in wet strands round her face, and her head-to-toe black outfit made her look more Gothlike than ever. Only Nesta didn't look like an iceberg, but maybe that's because being half-Jamaican, half-Italian, her fudge-colored skin doesn't fade to lily white like the rest of ours in the English winter.

As Nesta and I went inside the house, Lucy and Izzie were hauled off by the dogs in the direction of the café. Once we got in, however, Nesta spotted the room to the right of the entrance hall.

"Just a quick look," she said as she made a beeline for the gift shop where she spent fifteen minutes smelling all the bath gels on sale and then trying all the lip balms. She finally settled for a cherry-flavored one.

"We don't need to go round the house," she said as she gave the lady at the counter her money. "There are loads of books here that tell you all about the place and have photos of the rooms. We can have a quick flick through and we'll have seen all that there is here easy-peasy and without having to trudge round."

I give up, I thought. I like to go from room to room and sit and look at the paintings and soak up the atmosphere. Not much chance of that with Nesta, I don't think.

"Okay, quick flick through the books then we'll join the others," I agreed.

"Cool," said Nesta.

It was then she spotted the guest book and began to write in it. I went to sign my name after hers and saw what she had written.

"Queen Victoria was 'ere with her husband. We woz not amused."

If you can't beat them, join them, I thought as I wrote, "Kenwood rocks, signed Mick Jagger" underneath Nesta's writing.

Chapter 2

Dog Heaven

Hampstead Heath is dog heaven. Miles and miles of grounds and woodland for them to run about in while their owners collapse on benches and watch them work off their boundless energy. The rain had stopped, so we let Ben, Jerry, and Mojo off their leads and away they were, tails wagging, tongues out, grinning all over their faces as they greeted other dogs. And their owners.

"Pretend they're not with us," said Lucy as Ben enthusiastically sniffed the bottom of a rather surprised-looking poodle.

As we sat overlooking the hill rolling down to the lake at the bottom of the field, our conversation soon turned to one of our favorite subjects. Boys. Although we all have different interests, Izzie into all her New Age stuff, Lucy into fashion, Nesta into acting, and me into books and writing, we have one thing in common: the subject of boys and relationships.

"Luke's taking me to see some weird arty film tonight," said Nesta. "*Seven Samurai*, I think it's called. Supposed to be a classic."

"It is. You'll love it," I said. "It was remade later into *The Magnificent Seven*—you know, the cowboy film."

Nesta stared at me in amazement. "See. There you go again. Something else you seem to know all about and I've never heard off. And seeing as my dad's a film director, if anyone should know about movies, it's me. You're awesome, T. J. How come you *know* this stuff?"

I shrugged. "My brother Paul went through a phase when he was into all those old films. He never stopped talking about them. But I don't know loads of stuff. Honest. I'm not a Norma Know-It-All or anything."

Lucy put her hand on my arm. "We don't think you are," she said.

"No, just a—," started Izzie.

"Neoclassical wombat," Lucy finished for her.

"But hey, T. J.," said Nesta. "You shouldn't try and hide that you know loads or apologize about it. I'd be proud of it if I were you."

I grinned sheepishly. I've only been hanging

around with Nesta, Izzie, and Lucy since June. They adopted me after my best friend, Hannah, went to live in South Africa leaving me here on my own. They've been great mates and I really want to stay in with them. I don't want to make them feel like I'm showing off or anything, like trying to prove that I know more than them. I've got an uncle like that. Whenever anyone mentions any subject—politics, religion, books, whatever—he has to let everyone know that he's better informed than the rest of us, usually by giving us a ten-minute lecture. He's *really* boring, like his opinion is the only one that matters and the rest of us should be honored that he takes the time to fill us in.

"So when's your sister getting married, T. J.?" asked Lucy.

"Christmas Eve," I replied.

"That's *so* romantic."

"Nah. It's the only night Marie can get off from the hospital where she works," I said.

"I'd love to design a winter wedding gown," continued Lucy. "I've always envisaged a white velvet one with a long cloak." Lucy wants to design clothes when she leaves school. She has a great eye for fashion and has made some fab outfits. Shame she's not making my sister Marie's dress. Marie isn't romantic at all. She's totally disinterested and hasn't even been for a dress fitting yet.

"Oh, I'll just dash out and buy any old thing nearer the day," she said last time she was up from Devon, where she's started a new job so that she could be near her fiancé, Stuart. "I'm *so* not into having a white wedding. What's the point of forking out a fortune for some bit of fabric that you're only going to wear on one day."

"You will *not* dash out and buy any old thing," said Mum. "It's your big day and you're going to look fabulous whether you like it or not."

I laughed at the time and wondered whose big day it was really going to be, Mum's or Marie's. Either way, we're all going down south next weekend to, as Mum put it, "talk wedding dresses."

"Are they still arguing over whether to do it in a church or registry office?" asked Izzie.

I grimaced. Discussions had been going on for weeks now. "Yeah, and still nothing's been decided. Marie favors a registry office, but she has got some place she wants to show us for the reception. Mum and Dad want her to do it in a church. And Paul thinks she should never have told anyone about it and flown off to Hawaii in secret to get married on a beach, barefoot under the stars with some aging hippie type conducting a service that they'd written themselves."

"That sounds fab," said Izzie. "Your brother has the right idea."

"I read about a couple that got married at the

bottom of the sea, in scuba-diving outfits," said Nesta.

"Did they have a dolphin doing the service instead of the priest?" I asked.

"Or a whale?" asked Lucy. "Then they could have sent invites saying, Have a whale of a time at our wedding."

"Keep taking the tablets, Lucy," said Izzie.

"You can do anything you want these days," said Nesta. "Get married bungee jumping if you like."

"No, thanks," I said. "I think taking the leap to get married would be scary enough, never mind having to jump off a bridge into the bargain. Anyway, we're going down to discuss it all next weekend."

"It is a big commitment," said Nesta. "I mean, saying 'I do' to one person for the rest of your life. Like, how exactly do you know if he's The One?"

"Or number thirty-one?" said Izzie. "In your case, with the way you go through boys, that's probably the number you'll be on by the time you get to Marie's age. Twenty-six isn't she, T. J.?"

I nodded.

Nesta pinched Izzie's arm. "Cheek. I haven't had many boyfriends."

"More than the rest of us," said Lucy.

"Not *serious* ones," said Nesta. "Not like Luke."

"What about Simon?" said Izzie.

"Simon was okay, but it's different with Luke. We're really in love."

13

"How do you know that?" asked Izzie. "How do you know when it's really love? I mean, do you want to marry him?"

"Give me a break," said Nesta, laughing. "I'm only fifteen. And you don't want to marry everyone you love."

"In some cultures, girls marry or choose a partner when they're twelve . . . ," I started, then immediately regretted it.

"Yeah, you're right, in some cultures some girls get paired off really young," said Nesta.

"But you didn't answer my question," Izzie insisted. "How do you know when you're really in love? What do you think, T. J.?"

"Oh God. I don't know. Ask me when I'm older. When I've had a bit more experience. I've only had one proper boyfriend."

I've been dating Lucy's brother, Steve, for just over three months, and although I really like him, no way can I say that I'm in love. We like hanging out. Having a laugh. Lucy was looking at me curiously. Oh please don't ask me what I think you're going to ask me, I thought.

"So. Do you love Steve?" asked Nesta before Lucy could open her mouth.

"Er . . . we get on really well and . . ."

I think Lucy sensed my discomfort. "Don't embarrass her," she said.

"Okay, you then. Do you love Tony?" asked Nesta.

Lucy blushed. Tony is Nesta's elder brother, and he and Lucy have been seeing a lot of each other lately, although both of them insist that it's only casual.

"Dunno," she said. "I . . . like him more than any other boy that I've ever been out with. And as you all know, that's not many. Um. Two, in fact. So it's hard to tell. I like him a lot, but I always imagined that with true love, you'd really know it. Both of you. Not all this on-off stuff Tony and I do. Neither of us can make up our minds what we want."

"Oh, I think Tony knows exactly what he wants," said Nesta.

"Which is?" asked Lucy.

"To get you to do the horizontal shoe shuffle."

"*Whadttt?*" asked Lucy.

"You know, sex."

Lucy blushed furiously. "You're probably right," she said with a sigh. "But I'm sure if I did the, er . . . horizontal shoe shuffle, he'd lose interest in no time."

"Not necessarily," said Nesta.

"Oh, he would. Anyway, I'm not ready. I don't want to be pressured into it. I want to do it when the time feels right. It was enough worrying about whether I was a good kisser or not. I don't want to get into worrying about whether I'm good at sex, as well."

"I believe in soulmates," said Izzie. "That somewhere

on the planet is someone who is perfect for you and if you meet him, then sex and all the rest of it will be perfect and you won't have to worry."

"Somewhere on the planet?" I asked. "What if your soulmate lives in Outer Mongolia and you never meet?"

"I believe in soulmates as well," said Lucy, "and, if he lived somewhere remote, fate would bring you together, at an airport or somewhere, like two magnets drawn together irresistibly. You'd just be about to get on your plane to Paris, and he would be dashing down an escalator, and your eyes would meet . . ."

"And he'd trip and fall over someone's suitcase," said Izzie, "bang his head, and when he woke up, you'd be standing over him . . ."

"With choirs of heavenly angels singing hallelujah," I added laughing. "Oh, get real, guys. You've all been watching way too many slushy films."

"Well, maybe not like that," said Lucy. "But I reckon that if you met your soulmate, there would be some kind of recognition. You'd be on the same wavelength and maybe even know what each other was thinking without having to say anything."

"Maybe," said Nesta, "but who's to say you only have one soulmate? You might have loads."

"You wish," said Lucy. "I read somewhere that soulmates have been together through many lifetimes. So I think that Izzie is right, there would be some kind of recognition. It would be like meeting a long lost friend and there would be something familiar about them, because actually you've been together time after time."

"God, I hope not," said Nesta. "Sounds awful. I mean marriage to one person sounds bad enough, but a whole eternity with the same guy. You'd have to love him one heck of a lot. Whatever happened to having fun? Never mind finding Mr. Right. I'll settle for Mr. Right Now."

"If it's meant to be," said Izzie, "it's meant to be."

Nesta pulled a doubtful face. "Hmm. You'd have to believe in reincarnation and I'm not sure I do. Only way to know is die and find out. Then you'll know for sure. Like with soulmates, if I meet one, I'll let you know."

"I agree," I said. "I think the notion of soulmates is just a romantic way of saying that there are some boys you click with or fancy more than others. End of story."

"Well, I hope you meet your soulmate in *this* life," said Izzie. "Then you'll be proved wrong."

"Yeah, right," I replied with a grin.

"But nobody has answered Izzie's question," said Lucy. "How do you know if you're really in love?"

"Can't sleep. Can't eat. It's like having a nasty virus and feeling insane," said Izzie. "That's why I like being celibate. It's nice. Peaceful. No having to worry about will he phone me. Is my bum too big and all that crapola."

I cracked up. "How can you be celibate when you haven't even had sex yet?"

"Easy. Celibate means an unmarried person or someone who isn't having sex," said Izzie. "So I've been celibate for fifteen years now. But going back to love, I reckon it does your head in. All the great love songs say so. Like having an itch that you can't scratch. The love bug. I got a fever, et cetera, et cetera. Count me out."

Lucy nodded. "But it's a nice itch."

"Yeah," agreed Nesta. "Like you can't stop thinking about him. Can't wait to be with him. Time is slow when you're apart, yet it passes quickly when you're together. It's like that with Luke."

"Bit of an old romantic yourself, eh, Nesta," I teased. I hoped nobody would ask me about being in love with Steve again. I mean, I really liked him, but there was no way I thought about him *all* the time.

"I think you know it's love because you feel all tingly when you're with him," said Lucy. "Like you're really alive, energized."

"You can get that feeling from drinking a drink from the health shop," said Izzie. "Try one with ginseng in it."

I laughed. "So who needs love?"

"I think that if you meet The One then you'd be able to be your best self with him," said Lucy. "Talk to him. It would feel right, easy. You'd be able to be yourself without having to put on an act or feeling like you have to impress him."

"That sounds cool," I said. "I reckon Mojo must be The One then, because that's how I feel around him. I can talk to him about anything, and he always looks really interested."

"I said you were weird," said Izzie. "But seriously, this One. Would he be like you, with lots in common? Or would it be a case of opposites attract?"

"Maybe it's just chemical," I said as I watched Mojo chasing a border collie, then do the doggie "hi" by smelling its rear end. "Pheromones. Purely animal. Like dogs. You like the way they smell."

Nesta laughed as she watched the dogs. "Imagine if we did that! It would be hysterical. No way am I going round smelling bottoms. Not very romantic! There has to be a more dignified way to know if he's The One."

"I guess we'll know whether it's love when the time comes," I said.

"Yeah," said Izzie. "Like when it's hot or cold. You just know it."

"And in the meantime, we can have lots of fun along the way," said Nesta.

Around lunchtime, we rounded up the dogs and tied their leads to our bench. I stayed to keep an eye on them to make sure that they didn't drag the bench down the hill while the others went to the ladies' room.

"So how was that?" I asked Mojo, who was sitting at my feet looking up at me adoringly. "Did you make any new friends?"

"First sign of madness, talking to yourself," said a male voice to my right.

I looked up to see Nesta's boyfriend smiling down at me.

"Er, nihi . . . I was talking to my dog," I blustered.

"Oh. He speaks English, does he?"

I laughed. "Do you know that had never occurred to me. Maybe I ought to try French?"

"Or Italian," added Luke, laughing, and leaned over to say something to Mojo in Italian. Mojo leaped up, put his paws on Luke's shoulders, and licked his face with great enthusiasm.

"Omigod," I said. "I think you might be right. Mojo is clearly Italian. Oh, no. Now I'll have to learn how to speak it."

Luke laughed again. "Hey, is Nesta with you? She called me on her mobile and asked me to meet her here."

I jerked my thumb toward the ladies' room. "She'll be back in a mo."

Luke sat down beside me and turned to look at the house on the right, behind us. "Did you go inside?"

"Only for a minute," I said. "None of the others were too keen. I'm going to come back and do it properly another day. I love looking round places like this."

"Me too," said Luke. "It's one of my favorite things. I like imagining what the people were like who lived here. . . ."

"Me *too*," I said. "Yeah. Like who were they? Were they happy?"

"Yeah. Did they get on? Have kids? Is there a good vibe or a bad vibe in there? I like reading books about places like this; sometimes they have photos of the inhabitants and their families. As I look at their faces, I wonder, What were you thinking the day you were painted? Like, what did you have for breakfast?"

"*Yeah*. I like to sit and soak up the atmosphere, see if I can somehow be transported back. . . ."

"Yeah," said Luke. "And don't you think it's amazing that this place is here? Some people go all the way to Paris or Rome to see works of art and we have some amazing ones right on our doorstep."

I turned and had a good look at him. I couldn't believe he was saying exactly what I thought. I'd only met Luke once before, and then it was only briefly with a crowd of others at his parents' restaurant. They're Italian and knew Nesta's dad when they were younger, and there was some drama going on about a falling-out they had years ago, and Nesta was told she couldn't see Luke. All sorted now, but I hadn't really talked to him as it was neither the time nor place. Or looked at him beyond a glance. And now that I did look, there was something about him that looked . . . sort of familiar. I felt myself flush as he looked back at me.

"Have we met before?" he asked.

I nodded. "Yeah. With Nesta at your parents' restaurant."

He shook his head. "No. Before then. I remember *that* night. No. It's just . . . you look kind of familiar."

I shook my head. "No, I don't think so." I would have remembered meeting someone as striking as Luke. He wasn't your average tall, dark, and handsome, although he was all of those things with a mane of black hair. It made him look like a poet from a bygone era. But there was something else about him. He looked interesting. Intelligent. He was still staring at me, and I felt myself turning pink. I stood up and started playing with the dog's lead. When I looked at Luke again, he was smiling, like he was amused. Was it because he'd felt my embarrassment and was laughing at me? He probably had this effect on loads of girls. Or was he amused because I'd got the dogs' leads all tangled and almost tripped over Jerry? Oh, hell. Whatever, I thought. Nesta's lucky to have such a gorgeous boyfriend. I'd love to talk to him more about old houses and paintings. I glanced at him again as he kneeled on the ground by the bench and tried to untangle the leads.

"I'd love to talk to you more some day about old houses," he said as he looked at me. "Not many people are that interested."

I gulped. "Er nihi . . . ," I muttered as Izzie, Nesta, and Lucy came bouncing up the steps behind us and put an end to our conversation.

Meeting The One

Who says you get only one One? If you're lucky, you will meet The One, The Two, The Three . . . and so on. —Nesta

The One will be your soulmate for life. —Lucy

If it's meant to be, destiny will bring you together in this life as it has in past lives. —Izzie

It's all chemical. The One is just a way of saying you fancy someone and your pheromones are mutually attractive. —T. J.

Chapter 3

Our Father
Who Art in
Devon

"Typical Marie," said Mum as we drove down to Devon the following Saturday. "She always was a contrary one."

"I thought Paul was your difficult child, Mum," I teased from the back. My brother Paul freaked my parents out in the summer by dropping out of medical school to travel the world. He's in Morocco at the moment and flying back on Christmas Eve for the wedding before going on to Ethiopia in the New Year. Dad calls him a drifter as he hasn't decided what he wants to be yet.

"You're *all* difficult," said Dad as he steered our car

down the A–381 toward a place called Bigbury Bay in Devon.

"But honestly, a *sea* tractor!" said Mum. "What is the girl thinking of?"

"Well, we'll have a look and try to talk her out of it," said Dad. "You know, take the line of going along with it all, then try to make her see sense."

I thought the location sounded fab and wondered if I should warn Marie about their "let's go along with it" strategy. Apparently Marie's found this hotel on an island that caters for weddings and the only way to get to it, when the tide is in, is by sea tractor. Excellent, I thought when I heard the news. Makes a change from arriving at a wedding in the usual boring limo.

Mum hadn't finished her rant. "How on *earth* does she think she's going to get all the guests across to the hotel? No. The idea is ridiculous."

"It was good enough for royalty," I said. I'd looked the place up on the Internet last night. It sounded just my kind of thing, an old hotel steeped in history. Apparently anyone who was anyone used to go there in the summers of the 1930s. Edward, Prince of Wales; Mrs. Simpson; Noel Coward; Amy Johnson; Winston Churchill to name a few. According to the Web site, it was flapper heaven with an orchestra playing on a platform in a natural swimming pool called the Mermaid Pool.

But on they went, moan, moan, moan. I tried making them laugh with Lucy's joke, our father who art in Devon, Harold be thy name, but they didn't find it funny. No, they were having much more fun having a groan.

"London would have been much more convenient for the guests from the north," said Mum.

"And what if the weather's bad? It will be a nightmare if no one can get there," said Dad. "No. It doesn't bode well."

"And it's not cheap either," said Mum.

I decided to close my eyes and try and sleep. Burgh Island Hotel sounded the business to me, and anyway, it was Marie's wedding not Mum's or Dad's. As I drifted off, I found myself thinking about Luke. I wonder if he knows about this place. Sounds like his sort of thing too. He's been popping into my head all week, on and off. I kept replaying the moment he turned and asked if we'd met before over and over in my head. It was amazing, as usually when I meet a good-looking boy, my brain turns to mush and my vocal cords paralyze. I get taken over by this alien girl I call Noola who can't say anything except *uhyuh, yuneewee,* and *nihingyah.* But I'd managed to have a conversation with Luke. Actually spoken words that formed themselves into meaningful sentences. It was like I'd known him for ages. And the moment he talked to Mojo in Italian—it was so funny. . . . But I mustn't think about him. He's Nesta's boyfriend. Steve. *Steve* is my boyfriend. I ought to be daydreaming about telling him about Burgh Island, not Luke. He likes places with interesting histories too. So why didn't you think of telling *him* about it first? asked a prissy voice in the back of my head. He's not as good-looking as Luke, said another voice. Steve is cute in his own way. He looks like an eighteen-year-old Harry Potter, whereas Luke is a total babe with his wide mouth, thick eyelashes, and . . . oh shut up, I thought. Shut up, shut up, shut up. I made a resolution to tell Steve all about Burgh Island the moment I got back.

Mum and Dad's moaning and groaning continued as we parked in the car park on the mainland opposite the hotel and unloaded our overnight bags from the trunk. I looked across the bay and there was the hotel, exactly as the Web site had described it: "A white art deco cruise liner beached on dry land." I couldn't wait to get there.

The sea tractor was brilliant. I'd never seen anything like it. It was like traveling on an open-air bus with ginormous wheels, and before we knew it, we were across the bay and a man was taking our bags and loading them in a car to drive us the short distance up to the hotel.

"All this palaver," Mum droned on as we passed a

little pub called the Pilchard Inn. "And what if it snows?"

We'd been in the hotel about five minutes, and I could see that Mum and Dad's objections were fading fast.

"Well, I suppose it is rather nice when you get here," said Mum as she took in the fabulous art deco interior.

"Hmm," said Dad approvingly as he strolled into a room called the Palm Court that had a stunning domed, stained-glass roof in vibrant peacock colors.

"*Nice?* Mum, it's awesome," I said as Marie came out from the Palm Court to meet us.

"Awesome," she said. "I take it that you approve then?"

"I do," I said.

"What about the wrinklies?" she whispered after hugs and enquiries about the journey, and Mum and Dad busied themselves with signing in and getting our room keys.

I laughed. Marie's picked up on my nickname for Mum and Dad. I started calling them the wrinklies because they're so much older than most people's parents. Probably not for Marie and Paul as they're both in their twenties, but I came along later. A surprise baby I think I was. Probably *was* a surprise as both Mum and Dad are doctors and should know better about contraception and the like. It was funny when Mum gave me my first "sex" talk and lectured me about, "How it can only take one time" and, "Mistakes do happen." I asked her if I was a mistake, and she didn't know where to look.

"They'll be okay," I said. "Just give them time."

After a fabulous lunch in the Sun Lounge, Mum and Dad seemed to be doing a total about-turn.

"Winston Churchill came here, you know," said Dad as he puffed on a cigar.

Mum sipped her coffee. "And Edward, Prince of Wales, and Mrs. Simpson."

Dad smiled. "You can almost see them in their whites, can't you? Running through the corridors calling 'Anyone for tennis' to each other."

"And Agatha Christie wrote here," I added. "In fact, it was used as a location for the film *Evil Under the Sun.*"

Mum sighed contentedly and looked out of the window. "It *is* lovely. How did you find it, Marie?"

"Stuart brought me here last month, and we both fell in love with the place," said Marie. "Then when we realized that they had a license to do weddings, well . . ."

Hah. I thought. Sorted. Everybody happy.

"Just don't make me wear pink on the day," I said.

Marie laughed. "Oh, I thought a bright *candy* pink might be nice. With lots of ribbons and bows.

Gimme a break. You can be my bridesmaid in your jeans and trainers. As long as you're here, that's all I care about."

"Talking of outfits," said Mum, rooting in her bag and producing a wad of brides' magazines, "I brought these for us to look through."

Nice try, I thought as I looked at Marie sympathetically.

A little later, we went back over to the mainland, and that's when the real trouble started. It was a lovely afternoon with a bright blue sky, and Marie drove us around the area. It was incredibly pretty. Idyllic, in fact. Thatched cottages, winding roads through hedgerows, quaint little villages. After a stop for a cup of tea in a roadside tea shop, Marie set off to find a bank, and Mum and Dad headed down the High Street and started gazing in estate agents' windows.

"What are you looking for?" I asked as I caught up to them. "Somewhere to rent for the summer?"

Mum glanced at Dad. "Er, not exactly," she said.

"Just getting an idea of the prices," said Dad as he continued looking in the window.

"Why? Are you thinking of going into real estate?" I asked.

"No," said Dad and looked at Mum. "Um. Er. You tell her, Maureen."

Mum took a deep breath. "We've been meaning

to talk to you about it for some time, T. J. We've been thinking of moving."

"Moving! Why? When? What for?"

"Now, don't panic," said Mum. "Actually, we've been talking about it for some time now. . . ."

"Not to me, you haven't. This is the first I've heard."

"We didn't want to say anything until we were more sure, but your father is thinking of going part-time and commuting. We've always liked this part of the world and after looking around today, well . . ."

"But why can't you go part-time and stay in London, Dad?"

"We could. That is . . . was an option. But we fancy a change of pace. And it won't be long before we come up for retirement. We always wanted to retire by the sea, and now that Marie's down here as well . . ."

Noooooooooooooooooooooooooooooooooooooo, I thought as alarm hit the pit of my stomach. "But what about me? What about school? What about my friends?"

Dad hesitated for a while. "A change of pace might do you good as well," he said finally. "I'm not sure that London's the best place for you and . . . well, that new crowd you've got in with . . ."

"New crowd? You mean, Lucy, Nesta, and Izzie? But you hardly know them. . . ." He didn't either as

I hardly ever took them back to my house. Dad never liked me bringing friends home that much and when I did, he always complained about the noise. It was much simpler to go and hang out at their houses.

"I do know them, T. J. What about that time I caught you all having a pillow fight and jumping up and down on your bed? Not very mature. Not the behavior of nice young ladies. You're going to be fifteen on Monday, and it's time you started acting your age."

"But we were just being silly that day. We're not usually like that."

"What about that Izzie, then? Remember that incident with her? I think she might be a bad influence."

"*Izzie!* But . . . why Izzie?"

"Even her own mother was worried about her in the summer. She was round at our house, and she'd been out with some strange boy and drinking. . . ."

I snorted back laughter. "That was a one-off. Izzie is Queen Organic. She's so into health stuff. Honestly. She's *not* a bad influence. No way. I could show you girls at our school who are a bad influence, but not Izzie."

Wrong thing to say.

"Exactly," said Dad. "So you admit that there are girls at your school who are a bad influence?"

"No. Yes. But I don't hang with them. No. Mum. Dad. No. We can't move. My whole life is up in London. I *can't* leave."

But Mum and Dad had spotted another estate agent's on the opposite side of the road and were making a beeline for it.

No. No. Noooooooooooooo, please God, I thought. I mean, I like Devon and all, but live here? Noooooooooooooooooooo.

Burgh Island Hotel is on Burgh Island, which is a twenty-six-acre tidal island, two hundred meters off the south Devon coast between Salcombe and Plymouth.

Famous people who have stayed there include Noel Coward; Agatha Christie; Edward, Prince of Wales; Mrs. Simpson; Amy Johnson; and Winston Churchill.

Movies in which it was used as a location include *Evil Under the Sun*.

Chapter 4

School
Project

"But you *can't* go," said Lucy as we went into assembly the following Monday. "Steve was gutted after you told him last night."

I stuffed the birthday cards and presents that they'd just given me into my rucksack. Lavender bath gel and soap from Nesta, glittery nail polish from Lucy, a scented candle from Izzie, plus Lucy had brought me a card and present from Steve—a CD collection of love songs from the last decade. Somehow, their gifts made the fact that I might have to move away even worse. Even though they were birthday presents, it felt like they were leaving presents.

"Never mind Steve," said Izzie linking her arm through mine. "I'm gutted. We'd really miss you."

"Maybe you could come back at weekends," said Nesta. "You can stay in my room with me."

"And we'd come down to visit in the holidays," said Lucy. "I like Devon."

"So do I," I said as we took our places in our class line up. "But that doesn't mean I want to live there." I felt utterly miserable. Some birthday, I thought. Fifteen and it felt like my life was over. I wouldn't know anyone in Devon. Starting a new school would be horrible, like reliving what it was like when Hannah first moved abroad. And I know what Hannah went through when she first got to South Africa, although she's made friends now. But I didn't want to make new friends. I didn't want to go through all that again. I liked Lucy, Izzie, and Nesta. I'd never find mates like them again. And no matter how much they insisted they'd come to visit and stay in touch, I knew what would happen. It was happening with Hannah already. We'd promised to e-mail every day, keep telling each other everything, but she hadn't been in touch for weeks now—not even an e-mail wishing me happy birthday. But come to think of it, I hadn't been in touch either. It was too awful to think that the same thing might happen with my new friends. No. Mum and Dad couldn't be serious. It was a mad idea.

"You could always run away," Nesta whispered in my ear. "We'd make sure you had food and stuff. . . ."

"Quiet at the back," called Mrs. Allen looking pointedly in our direction.

After the usual boring announcements, Mrs. Allen suddenly beamed. "Now, girls, I have something special to tell you about today. An exciting project is to be launched by the mayor, and it's one that I think many of you will be very interested in. . . ."

Nesta turned and feigned a yawn to me. I grinned back at her.

"The aim of the project is to produce a book detailing our city's heritage," continued Mrs. Allen, "that has been written and researched by the city's students. The final version is to go on sale at the British Museum. The project is open to all pupils from Year Ten and upward who wish to take part. The mayor has asked that those involved research London as it is today and London as it was in the past. Areas such as history, famous landmarks, build-ings, costumes through the ages, contributions from its inhabitants, artists, writers, architects . . . and the list goes on. Schools have been chosen from each of the four areas of London: North, South, East, and West. Our school has been fortunate enough to have been asked to be one of the schools representing the north. Each school within each area will obviously focus on their particular area. . . ."

Sounds brilliant, I thought. I'd love to be involved, but I'll probably be living out in the back of beyond in some backwater with people who've never even been to London.

"The mayor has asked to see an initial presentation just before Christmas, so that only gives us until the end of term," Mrs. Allen continued. "So we need to get ourselves in gear immediately. The first meeting for the North London area, for those of you who'd like to contribute, will be tomorrow evening at the Institute of Science in Pond Square in Highgate, so . . . all those budding journalists, historians, and artists out there, take note. All the head teachers of the schools taking part are meeting tonight, and we're going to appoint one pupil to oversee the project with the help of a number of teachers. But essentially, this is your project, and I hope that you will rise to meet the challenge and make this particular school proud of your efforts. At the end of term, there will be an open day featuring the work so far, and school governor, Susan Barratt, and celebrity journalist Sam Denham, whom I believe some of you know from his visit here last year, will be attending. Details have been posted on the notice board in the hall. Pupils involved will be given time to work on the project and can arrange this with their head of year."

Cool, I thought as Mrs. Allen continued. Even though we might move to Devon before the project is completed, Mum said it might be ages before they find the right house, so I've got at least one more term here, and then they've got to sell our house. I'd have time to take part in the initial stages at least.

"Well, you can count me out," said Nesta as we made our way to first lesson. "We get enough home-work as it is."

"Might be fun," said Lucy. "I'm going to volunteer. I could research costumes through the ages. It's an excuse to go and look round places like the Victoria and Albert Museum. I've been meaning to do it for ages, and you never know, it might give me inspiration for my own designs. I like combining the old with the new."

"What about you, T. J.?" asked Izzie. "You up for it?"

I nodded. "Think so. I'd like to do something on the old houses in Hampstead and Highgate. You know, like Kenwood House. There are plenty of other places I've been meaning to get round to. Like Lucy said, it's a good excuse to do it, and it might be my last chance if we move."

"And you could do something on the spiritual side of London," suggested Lucy, turning to Izzie.

"Maybe," she replied. "Yeah. I'll have a think about it."

Nesta pouted. "I hate you all. Now I feel left out, or at least I will if you all take part and I don't."

"Then choose something interesting to you," I

said. "You could look at theater through the ages. Or great love affairs."

Nesta didn't look convinced. "I guess," she said. "And Mrs. Allen did say that there'd be time off to do it. So maybe. Certainly no harm in going to the open day at the end of term. That Sam Denham was a bit of a dish. I wouldn't mind seeing him again."

I laughed. Typical Nesta, I thought as Lucy, Izzie, and I signed our names on the board and wrote our area of interest.

On Tuesday night, we met at Nesta's house near Highgate and got changed and made up.

"Just in case there are any boy babes there," said Izzie as she wriggled into a denim mini with a zip down the front.

"I thought you were going through a celibate phase," I said.

Izzie laughed. "I like to keep an open mind on all matters."

"And I've decided I'm not going to do it," said Nesta. "It's not my thing."

"So why are you coming?" I asked.

"Luke's going to be there. His school is one of the ones chosen as well."

"So is Steve's," I said. "He called earlier. He wants to do photography."

"What about Lal?" asked Izzie.

Lucy laughed. "Not interested. Too much like hard work, he said. What about Tony, Nesta?"

"His headmaster turned it down. Said that the pupils there had to focus on their exams. But then Luke's doing A-levels as well, but his headmaster didn't seem to mind. Apparently he said it would look good on their CV if their material gets used."

"More like the school's CV," I said. "Smart headmaster if you ask me."

The hall was already full when we got to the institute, and Nesta spied Luke on the other side of the room at the front. He gave us a friendly wave, and I watched as Nesta made her way over to him, and he put his arm around her and steered her toward a seat. He looked gorgeous in a big overcoat with a red scarf knotted round his neck. I looked around for Steve, but couldn't see him in the crowd.

The meeting soon got underway with one of the teachers from a school in Cricklewood taking the chair.

"My name's Miss Longbottom," she started, and immediately I noticed Lucy's shoulders begin to shake in front of me. It doesn't take a lot to make Lucy laugh, only trouble is that it's infectious. Especially in a place where you're not supposed to be laughing. Izzie's shoulders started to shake next, and I missed the list of categories that Miss Longbottom was reading out as I battled not to laugh as well. I caught the end of what she said, though. Some girl called Marie Nash was to be the overall coordinator, and the different areas of interest had their own coordinators who we were to report to.

Lucy took note of who was in charge of costume and who was in her group. Steve was put in charge of photography with a team of three other pupils, and Izzie was put with a boy called Trevor in charge of the spiritual development of North London. I wondered if he knew what he was in for. He looked very straight and probably envisaged looking at churches and the development of Christianity. With Izzie by his side, he'd be looking at witches, mysticism, and lines of energy if she had her way. There were other groups for science, music, geography, architecture, and finally Miss Longbottom got to the famous houses and their inhabitants.

"And now we come to the inhabitants and historical houses in North London. Luke De Biasi will be coordinating this area along with"—she glanced down at her list—"Theresa Joanne Watts, Sian Collins, and Olivia Jacobs.

Nesta turned and gave me the thumbs-up. I smiled back at her. Cool, I thought. I'll get a chance to talk to him properly about old houses.

"Okay, everyone," said Miss Longbottom, "now, if you can all divide into your areas and introduce yourselves, we'll reconvene in about twenty minutes."

As everyone got into groups, Nesta caught up with me as I made my way over to meet Luke, Olivia, and Sian.

"It's so top, you'll be working with Luke," she said. "You can keep an eye on those two other girls while you're at it. I saw the way that little blond one looked at him. I'm sure she fancies him."

"I don't think you've anything to worry about," I said as I glanced over, and Luke beckoned me to go and join them. "She's not a patch on you."

"Well, report back if there's any funny business, won't you?"

"Course I will," I said. "Just call me Spy Kid 3."

E-mail: **Outbox (1)**
From: babewithbrains@psnet.co.uk
To: hannahnutter@fastmail.com
Date: 25 November
Subject: Londres

Aloha, Hannah, ma petite fruitcake.

Sorry I haven't been in touch lately. It's been mad here. How you doing? I still miss you. Life is major crapola at the mo. Mum and Dad have had a nasty turn and decided they want to go and live in Devon. Yes, Devon. No thank you.

Still hanging with Izzie, Lucy, and Nesta. They are great mates, which will make it even harder if I have to leave London.

Cool news is that we're doing a big project (loads of schools involved) about London's history. I'll be working with Nesta's new boyfriend, Luke, who is a total dish. And really nice.

Luv,
T. J.

E-mail: **Inbox (1)**
From: <u>hannahnutter@fastmail.com</u>
To: <u>babewithbrains@psnet.co.uk</u>
Date: 25 November
Subject: Moving

Bernando fernando octiposie.

God! Poor vous. Major whammy in the problemo stakes.

Okay. Listen to Auntie Hannah.

Re: moving:

Plan A: When the estate agents send people to view your house, volunteer to show them round. As you do, let it slip that you have psychotic neighbors with very noisy children who all have criminal records.

Plan B: Tell prospective buyers that the house has a ghost. A really horrible ghost, who likes to wander round with an amputated arm and hit people with the soggy end. Tell them, he's 'armless enough apart from that one habit. Hahahahaha.

Plan C: Get a load of rotting garbage, hide it in every room, then tell the prospective buyers that there is a bad damp problem in the house.

That should sort them. Am I a genius or wot?

What happened to Steve? You didn't mention him. Are you still dating?

Over here we're going into summer sizzler time

and it's fab. It's probably no consolation, but remember how I felt when I heard we were moving. I thought my life was over. Now I love it here and have made good friends. Things change. You might actually like Devon. I know that's probably not what you want to hear at the moment, but things might not be as black as they seem.

Yours truly,
Agony Aunt Hannah
P.S.: Write back soon.
P.P.S.: Omigod. I've just seen the date and realized. It was von birthcake yesterday. Oh er. Bad girl, Hannah. Um. Card in the post. Present in the . . . in the shop. I am soooooo sorry. I will make it up to you. Please don't hate me forever. Happy, happy birthday even if it's late. And sorreee sorreeee sorreeee am bad friend. Smackgirlnaughty.

Please e-mail back instantly and say you forgive moi.

E-mail: **Outbox (1)**
From: babewithbrains@psnet.co.uk
To: hannahnutter@fastmail.com
Date: 26 November
Subject: Birthday

You ees forgiven. My birthday was no big deal this year. For one thing it was on a Monday and school day. Mum and Dad took me for a special cream tea when we were down in Devon, which was nice, but then I am anti-Devon at the mo (haha, you're Auntie Hannah, and I'm anti-Devon, geddit?) so couldn't really enjoy it. Got loads of fab pressies from the girls though and a lovely CD collection from Steve. Next year, however, I will be sixteen and expect you to fly over and make a personal appearance.

Love,
Anti Devon

Chapter 5

Funny
Business?

"So what role would you like me to play, Luke?"
asked Sian.

Luke looked thoughtful. "Hamlet," he said.

Sian threw her head back and snorted a weird
loud laugh. Like a donkey braying. Whoa, I thought.
What Luke said was funny, but not *that* funny.

We were having our first meeting the following
evening in one of the art prefabs at the back of our
school. It had been allocated as a make-do office for
our part of the project. It was lucky for me that it
was at our school as the others had to travel to different areas. Lucy to a school in Kilburn, and Izzie to
one in St. John's Wood.

Luke got up and stood on one of the desks. "So,"

he said, grinning down at the three of us. "Here we are, team. Without further ado, I now declare this meeting open."

He stepped down and the meeting got going. He'd clearly already put a lot of thought into it as he had leaflets, brochures, and details about old houses printed out from the Net.

"We have a huge area to cover, so I suggest that we break it down. If we focus on Hampstead and Highgate up to Christmas for the first presentation, that will give us lots to work with in the initial stages. We can do the rest of North London later. So. I'm going to allocate places for each of us to visit. Best we start this weekend as we don't have a huge amount of time. I suggest at this stage we visit the places, make our notes, then meet again early next week to see which we want to keep in and which we want to keep out.

"Okay, Kenwood House. Olivia, you take that one, okay?"

Olivia nodded and took the brochure that he handed her. I liked the look of her. She was tall and skinny with bright red hair cut in a short bob and was attractive, but not in the conventional sense, as she had a large nose, but it kind of fitted her face. I thought that if I was in her class at school, I'd have picked her to be a friend—she looked interesting.

"Sian, you can do Burgh House. It's at the back of

Hampstead village. I think you'll like it there."

Sian nodded. "Okay, boss." In contrast to Olivia, Sian was short and blonde. She had a thin face and a long body with a large bottom and short legs, typical pear shape. She seemed nice enough though, eager to get on with us all and to please. Especially Luke.

"Now, Miss T. J. Watts, or would you prefer me to call you Theresa Joanne?" asked Luke with a wicked smile.

"T. J. will do just fine, thank you very much," I said, sounding like a real priss queen. "Everyone calls me T. J."

"T. J. it is then," he said. "Now, where shall I send you?"

"I was looking on the Internet last night, and I found that there are loads of companies that do guided tours of the area. There's one leaving from Hampstead tube at two o'clock on Sunday. Might be worth doing as it sounds like they cover a lot of ground, and they'll probably be brill on the history of the area."

"Excellent," said Luke. "In fact, I'll come with you. I've heard about that walk and always meant to do it."

Sian looked disappointed. "Maybe we should all do it," she suggested.

Luke shook his head. "No, two of us will be enough."

I felt chuffed that he wanted to go with me, and I

might have imagined it, but Sian gave me a funny look and appeared to be going into a sulk. However, she seemed to shake off her mood, and the rest of the meeting was really productive.

"There's Avenue House on East End Road in East Finchley," said Olivia, "that might be worth a visit. It's an interesting old place with lovely gardens."

"And Lauderdale House in Highgate," I said. "And, of course, Highgate Cemetery. That's fabulous, and there are so many famous people buried there, including Karl Marx. In fact, some people say it's a communist plot."

Luke and Olivia laughed, but Sian looked at me as though I was mad. I don't think she got the joke.

"Excellent suggestions, T. J.," said Luke. "And we must include the house where the poet John Keats lived, and Fenton House at the top of Hampstead. Yeah, we're going to have our work cut out, but it's going to be great. Really interesting."

His enthusiasm was infectious, and I felt really pleased that he was our coordinator. Unlike poor Izzie. She'd been put with a boy called Trevor from Steve's school, who not only looked boring, but Steve told me that he really was. Izzie wasn't looking forward to spending much time with him.

At the end of the hour, we all had a good idea what we had to do, and I felt fired up to get started. I felt sure that we were in with a good chance of our contributions being used if we could present all our findings in an interesting manner. With Luke in charge, I didn't think that would be a problem.

As I wandered out to the gate with Olivia after the meeting, once again I thought how lucky Nesta was to have a boyfriend like Luke. Good-looking, a nice guy, and a born leader. We were going to be a good team. I could see already that Sian would do anything Luke asked, and Olivia was really cool.

"Luke seems like a laugh," I said as we went and stood at the bus stop.

"Oh, yeah, he is. He's always been fun," she replied.

"Oh, do you know him, I mean apart from . . . ?"

"Yeah. I've known him for ages. He used to live in the same street as us. He's a mate of my brother William."

"What's he really like, then? He seems very confident, you know, knows exactly what he wants."

Olivia shrugged. "Yes and no. He wasn't always like that," then she laughed. "Bit of a late developer, if you know what I mean."

I didn't. "No," I said.

"He was never such a looker. He's kind of grown into himself in the last few years, but back when he was thirteen or fourteen, he was a bit gawky and could never get off with anyone. But now he's a babe magnet. They're queuing up for him. And he loves it."

"Oh really?"

"Yeah. But he never stays with anyone that long."

"Really? Oh dear. He's going out with my mate."

"Oh God, sorry. Maybe I shouldn't have said anything. And who knows? Maybe he's grown up a bit. Like, who's to say when true love will strike? Just he messed a mate of mine around. I still don't know if she's really over him."

"God. Why are some guys like that? You know, notching up girls . . ."

"I reckon it's because of his dad."

"His *dad*? His dad wants him to have loads of girlfriends?"

"No, dummy," Olivia said, laughing. "It's like he's trying to prove something to himself. His dad is really heavy sometimes. I know because Luke takes refuge at our house with William. He reckons Luke's dad has knocked his confidence. Like nothing is ever good enough. If he gets an A, why hasn't he got an A plus sort of thing. Now Luke has discovered something that he excels in. Pulling girls. It's an area where his dad can't interfere. And he's going for the A star."

"So you're saying that underneath, Luke is insecure?"

"I guess," she said, then smiled, "but then aren't we all, dwahling?"

I laughed. I was about to say something back

when I realized that I'd left my rucksack behind.

"Oh bummer," I said as a bus came round the corner. "Forgot my rucksack."

"See you next week then," she called as she stuck out her hand to stop the bus.

When I got back to the art prefab, the door was locked. That's strange, I thought as I'd left before Luke and Sian. I knocked then peeked through the window and could see Luke and Sian sitting close together. Very close together. And Luke was holding Sian's hand. Luke looked up, saw me at the window, and his face clouded. A moment later, he came to the door with my rucksack.

"Forget this?" he asked as he handed it to me. It was very clear that he didn't want me going inside. He looked uncomfortable, like he couldn't wait to get rid of me and, behind him, Sian's face looked a picture of guilt.

"Er . . . thanks," I muttered, then dashed away.

Omigod, I thought. Poor Nesta. Oh, poor, poor Nesta.

On the bus, I agonized over whether to call Nesta immediately and tell her what I'd seen. But what had I seen? I felt confused, and I didn't want to stir trouble unnecessarily. I'd only been back home about ten minutes and was about to have supper when the phone went.

"T. J., it's for you. Shall I tell him to phone back later?" called Mum from the hall.

"Who is it?"

"Someone called Luke."

"No, I'll take it," I said. I got up immediately. Maybe I should confront him and see what he says, I thought as I dashed to the hall.

"Hi."

"Hey, T. J.," said Luke cheerily. "Just confirming Sunday. How about you come here to my house, and I'll drive us into Hampstead."

"Um, okay. Yeah."

"And . . . I wanted to put you in the picture about Sian."

"Oh. Yeah. Sian," I said, wondering how he was going to get out of it.

"Bit of a screwball, little Sian," said Luke. "A mixed-up kid. She wanted to talk to someone, and I guess I was nearest. I was trying to make her feel better."

"Oh, right," I said.

"I don't know what impression you got when you looked through the window . . ."

"I . . . er . . ."

"All innocent. At least it is on my part. Between you and me, she's got a bit of a crush on me. Don't really know what to do about it. Got any ideas?"

Well, at least he'd come clean, I thought.

"Dunno. Um. Wear a bag over your head."

Luke laughed. "And pick my nose. Reckon that will put her off?"

I laughed as well. "Maybe." I felt flattered that he'd opened up to me and wanted my advice. I liked that. Like in the meeting, whenever I made a suggestion, he made me feel as if my opinion mattered. On some projects I've worked on in the past, some people are only interested in what they have to contribute.

"And, hey, no need to tell Nesta about her. I don't want her causing any trouble. As I said, Sian's a bit mixed-up. She doesn't need anyone coming down heavy on her when there's nothing going on."

"Sure," I said.

"So. Just between us?" he asked.

"Just between us."

After he'd hung up, I felt relieved I didn't have to tell Nesta. She'd have confronted Sian for sure. And if there was nothing in it, no point. Luke sounded nice, like he wanted to help Sian but not upset Nesta at the same time.

Some Houses of Interest That Are Open to the Public
in the Hampstead and Highgate Area

1) Burgh House, New End Square, Hampstead, London. Built in 1704.

2) Fenton House, Windmill Hill, Hampstead, London. Built around 1693 (one of the earliest and largest houses in the area).

3) Kenwood House, Hampstead Heath, London. An original smaller building was remodeled into the existing one in the 1700s.

4) Avenue House, East End Road, East Finchley. Built in 1859.

5) Lauderdale House, Waterlow Park, Highgate. Built around 1580.

6) Keats House, Keats Grove, Hampstead, London. The poet John Keats lived there from 1818 until 1820.

Chapter 6

Guided Walk

"Exactly what I wanted!" said Steve as he pounced on a book in the local library in East Finchley after school on Friday.

I went and looked over his shoulder. It was a book with old pictures of how Hampstead village used to look at the beginning of the last century.

"Top," I said as I watched him flick through. "Why don't you borrow it, find the locations, then you can take some up to the minute photos of exactly the same places? Then exhibit them side by side so people can see the difference."

"Excellent idea," he said. "My team thought we might do some of the local characters, too, and show them alongside those of people from the past. You know, the lollipop lady, policemen . . ."

"Traffic wardens," I said. "You see them more than you do policemen. They always remind me of wasps hovering around waiting to strike and sting."

Steve laughed. "And they do sting, too. Mum got a ticket the other day. Cost her a fortune. She was major miffed."

"Must have been amazing in the old days," I said. "Imagine how it must have been before all the cars and traffic."

"Yeah," said Steve. "Must have been fab."

After we'd looked at photography books, we searched for other books about the area, and Steve found me one that listed all the famous writers and artists that had lived there.

"Just what I need," I said as I glanced through it.

"And if you can find the places where they lived," said Steve, "then I'll take photos of the houses for you. For instance, the painter, John Constable, lived in Hampstead, and I'm pretty sure I've seen one of those blue plaques they put up on the outside wall of the house to say someone famous lived there. I just can't remember where."

"He lived in two places in Hampstead, one of them is on Well Walk," I said as I leafed through the book. "And according to this, there are loads of other famous people who either lived there or wrote about it. I know Charles Dickens is one of them as I often pass the house where he stayed on my way up to Nesta's. Maybe there will be a plaque outside her house one day when she's famous. Nesta Williams lived here. Actress and general fabster."

"Don't sell yourself short. Maybe there'll be one outside your house," said Steve, "when you're a famous international journalist and novelist." Then he laughed. "Lal wanted to make some of those plaques and sell them at Christmas. His latest marketing idea. He wants to make them look the same as the genuine article, you know blue with white writing, but instead of them being made of plaster or whatever they use, he wants to make them out of some kind of self-adhesive thin plastic so that people can stick them on their inside walls."

"But if no one famous lived in your house, what's the point?"

"Ah, but that *is* the point, or so Lal says. They wouldn't be plaques commemorating famous people, they'd be tributes to us lesser people, and people could choose what was written, like, 'Mrs. Jones lived here, the best mum in the world.'"

"Or Lal Lovering lived here, he was a total nutter," I suggested.

"Er, no, I think Lal had something more like, 'Lal Lovering lived here, the world's greatest lover.' You know what he's like."

I laughed. "It is a brill idea. I'd buy some. One for Izzie saying, 'Mystic Iz lived here. Astrologer, witch, and seeker.' For Lucy, 'Dress designer extraordinaire.' And Nesta . . ."

"Show-off and drama queen," said Steve. Unlike most boys, he had never fallen for Nesta, whereas Lal had the most ginormous crush on her and went gaga whenever he saw her.

"She's not really a show-off," I said. "She's just . . . an extrovert."

"Yeah, right. A show-off," said Steve.

When we went our separate ways later on in the afternoon, my thoughts turned to Luke and how I'd thought how lucky Nesta was to have him as a boyfriend. I should have thought how lucky *I* was to have a boyfriend like Steve. He's so easy to be with, a real friend and I know he'd do anything for me, like with the project, he's so supportive and as interested in what I'm doing as he is in his own part.

On Sunday morning I felt nervous about going to meet Luke. I guess I was a little intimidated by him. I spent ages trying to decide what to wear, as I didn't want to look like I'd made too much effort, but I didn't want to look like I'd just crawled out of bed either. After trying on half my wardrobe, I settled on my usual uniform of jeans and a jumper. Really boring, I thought as I checked my watch and realized that I'd better get going. I put on my denim jacket and checked the mirror again. Too much denim, I decided and changed the denim jacket for my black one. God, I hate this, I thought. I can never get that "just threw it on and look fabulous" look that the others seem to have down pat. I always end up with the "just threw it on and look ordinary" look. My style is the no-style style. I'd be the perfect candidate for one of those before-and-after makeovers that they do in magazines, only I'd be the before. And my after would look the same. I rummaged around in my chest of drawers and found the rainbow striped hat and scarf set that Marie bought me last Christmas. Hmm, brightens me up a bit, I thought as I checked the mirror again, but now I look like one of those cheery people who present children's programs on telly and dress in really bright colors. Too bad, I thought as I headed for the door. I'll have to do. And why am I even worrying about impressing Luke, anyway? With a girl-friend as stunning as Nesta, I don't reckon he even notices other girls, never mind what they're wearing.

I arrived about ten minutes early at the road where Luke lives. I didn't want to seem too eager so I stepped into a phone box to kill some time and reapply my lip gloss. After a while, I felt like a stalker watching his house from the phone box, so I took a deep breath and walked to his gate, up the path, and rang the bell.

"Be right there," called a voice from somewhere inside. A few moments later, Luke opened the door. "Come on in, I'm in the kitchen."

He led me through to the back of the house where he resumed ironing a shirt.

"Want anything to drink before we go?" he asked as he whipped off the T-shirt he had on.

Wow*zola,* I thought as I looked at his naked torso. I felt like Jim Carrey in that film *The Mask* when he sees Cameron Diaz for the first time and his eyes be-doiing out of their sockets and on to the floor and back again like they're on springs. *Then* I realized I was staring, so quickly looked at the door. Then I realized I might look seriously uncool, like I'd never seen a boy without his shirt on before. I was sure I was blushing. I made myself look up and meet his eyes. "Unyah, na, nah, no thanks," I stuttered. He had a fab body. And I mean *fab,* like he regularly worked out. His shoulders were broad, his skin a lovely olive color, and his upper chest was nicely toned, not muscley just . . . perfect. I've seen my brother Paul loads of times running around in his boxers, but he's a skinny thing, and his chest kind of sinks in. I've even seen Steve almost naked when he's been changing for tennis—to say that he's not a contestant for the Mr. Universe competition is an understatement, as he's kind of thin in the chest region, like Paul, and he's very, very pale. But Luke—he was like one of those Calvin Klein models modeling underwear that you see on posters on the sides of buses sometimes. As Izzie would say, hubba hubba. Get a grip, I told myself. You're acting like a stupid teenage schoolgirl. But I *am* a stupid teenage schoolgirl, said a voice in my head.

"Won't be a mo," said Luke as he donned the ironed shirt, then grabbed his big overcoat and scarf from the back of the kitchen door. "Okay, Watts, let's get ready to rumble."

"Er, right, rumble," I said as I followed him out through the house and to his car.

We arrived in Hampstead about fifteen minutes later and made our way up to the tube station.

"I'm really looking forward to this," said Luke as we joined a small crowd of tourists buying tickets from a man with a shaved head outside the tube. There was the usual bunch by the sound of their voices—a couple of Americans, a couple of Japanese, a couple of Australian students, a couple of Germans.

After a few minutes, more tourists poured out of the tube station, paid their money, and we were away.

"My name's Peter, and I'm your guide for the day," said the man with the tickets as he headed toward the traffic lights. "The tour will last about two hours. Now stick together and careful crossing the road. . . ."

"I feel like a kid in junior school," I whispered to Luke as the group of about twenty of us swarmed after him across the road.

"I know," laughed Luke. "And make sure you wipe your nose before you talk to anyone."

I was just about to get a tissue out when I realized that he was joking. Get a *grip*, Watts, I told myself. You're acting like a no-brain.

The tour was fascinating from the beginning when Peter told us that the name Hampstead came from a word that meant the old homestead when there was nothing but a farm in the area. It became more popular later when people used to come up to the area for the clean air and the waters.

"Both polluted now," laughed Luke as an old van spluttered past blowing fumes out of its exhaust pipe.

"Even King Henry the Eighth made use of the waters here," continued Peter. "He had all his laundry sent here, and the royal undergarments could be seen for miles drying on gorse bushes. The popularity of the waters and the area waned after a doctor declared that actually sea air was the best, and everyone took off for the coast. After that, the area became very popular with artists and writers. . . ."

Both Luke and I had to scribble notes madly to get down what Peter said as he led us down a lovely street full of Georgian houses called Church Row, named so because there was a church at the end of it. We had a quick look round the church, then went out into an old graveyard. This doesn't feel like

London at all, I thought as we strolled amongst the trees and old graves that were overgrown with ivy.

"This doesn't feel like London at all," said Luke. "It feels like the countryside."

"Just what I was thinking," I said.

"Go to the far end of the cemetery," said Peter pointing to a quiet corner, "and you'll see the grave of one of Hampstead's most famous residents."

The group moved over to where he had indicated under the trees, and there, to my amazement, was a raised large stone coffin on the side of which were engraved the words "John Constable."

I felt inexplicably moved. "I can't believe it," I said. "It's so unostentatious. No signs, no notices saying who's here. It makes it so much more impressive just to come across it. I'd have thought a painter as famous as he is would have been buried in one of the grander cemeteries or in a cathedral with a huge gold plaque."

Luke nodded. "Just what I was thinking."

"Great minds think alike." I grinned back at him.

"Constable painted the Heath more than any of the other painters who came here," said Peter. "He really loved the place."

"Kind of right that he should be buried here, then," Luke whispered to me.

After the graveyard at the back of the church, Peter led us over the road to another part of the cemetery. "It's claimed that the writer Jackie Collins and her sister, Joan, have already bought plots to be buried in here."

"No doubt Jackie'll have 'A plot at last' written on her gravestone."

Luke laughed. "I never realized that people could reserve where they wanted to be buried, though."

"Yeah. It's kind of morbid, don't you think? You know, planning your death?"

Luke nodded. "Yeah, but I guess it's going to happen to all of us at some time or other. Probably not a bad idea to think about how you'd want your send off to be."

"I'd like a choir singing something cheery, like, 'Wish Me Luck as You Wave Me Good-Bye,'" I said.

Luke laughed again. "I might have 'Cold As Ice,' or something appropriate like that. Or maybe 'Voodoo Child.' And afterward, I'd like to be stuffed and put in the corner of someone's hall and used as a hatstand."

I pinched his arm. "*Stop* it. I'm sure you'd make a very nice hatstand, but it's too spooky talking about death in a graveyard."

"They say that D. H. Lawrence's wife had him cremated, then mixed his ashes with concrete-type stuff and had him made into a fireplace."

"No way!"

"I read it somewhere, I swear," said Luke.

As we wandered through the back lanes, we

learned so much from Peter about the previous inhabitants of Hampstead: John Constable, George Du Maurier, George Romney. But it was also rumored that Russell Crowe had bought a house in the back lanes just round the corner from the director Ridley Scott, and the famous chef Jamie Oliver lived next door to the Holly Bush pub.

"Don't know if they're still here," said Peter, "as I'm not from this area, and it could just be gossip."

I couldn't wait to tell Nesta. Even if it was just a rumor that Russell Crowe was in the neighborhood, she'd still want to come and have a look. I felt a twinge of sadness about the imminent move to Devon as we wandered on. North London was so full of interest, and I'd be leaving it all behind me when there was still so much I wanted to explore.

At the top of Holly Hill, we stopped outside a grand-looking house called Fenton House. "This is one of the earliest houses in Hampstead, built in 1693," said Peter. "Now, have you noticed anything odd about the windows?"

"Some of them are bricked up," said one of the American tourists.

"Anyone know why?" asked Peter.

I put my hand up. "Um . . . in the sixteen hundreds, a tax was declared saying that the more windows you had, the more tax you had to pay. A lot of residents didn't want to pay the extra taxes and had their windows bricked up. They declared the tax as robbery, daylight robbery."

"Hence the origin of the saying that is part of our language today," said Peter. "Well done. Couldn't have put it better myself. It was during the reign of Queen Anne."

"Show-off," whispered Luke, then he pinched my arm and grinned. "I love finding out about things like that."

"Me too," I agreed.

Up and down and round the lanes we walked as Peter filled us in on history interspersed with gossip. "The pond at the top of Hampstead was where travelers used to stop to water their horses on their way in and out of London," he informed us. "It was also where highway men used to hide, so that they could pounce on the travelers as they tended their horses. It is said that Dick Turpin was one of them, and to this day he haunts the Spaniard's Inn just down the lane. The pond area was also where highwaymen were hanged as examples to others."

"Do you think that's where the term hanging out came from?" asked Luke.

I laughed. "Doubt it somehow. Maybe the expression 'hanging out to dry' is more like it."

As we proceeded down past the pond and into East Heath Road, there was a house where Elizabeth Taylor lived with Richard Burton; over the road from them, a fab Gothic mansion where Boy George used to live. I made a note to ask Steve to come and take photos of them for the open-day presentation.

Luke and I chatted easily as we followed everyone round and discovered that we had loads in common: books, our interest in history, old films, theater. At one point, he took my hand to lead me across a road and, for a moment, I let myself imagine what it would be like if he were my boyfriend. It was only for a moment, then I felt really bad. He was Nesta's boyfriend. How could I even consider it, even for a second? Plus Steve. I had Steve. I don't think he'd be too happy if he'd been passing and seen me holding Luke's hand, no matter how innocent.

"So you're dating Lucy's brother?" Luke asked as if he'd picked up on my thoughts once again.

I took my hand out of his immediately. "Um yes. Since the summer."

"I've seen him around, but never really spoken to him. What's he like?"

"Nice. Sweet. He's a real mate."

"Sweet, huh?" Luke gave me a strange look as if he were waiting for more, but I didn't feel comfortable talking to him about Steve. Instead I pretended I wanted to hear something that Peter was saying to one of the Japanese tourists and moved away from Luke.

The tour finished off as we walked down Well

Walk, which we learned was so named because that was where the wells of water used to be. Then on to Flask Walk, which is where the water was put into flasks to be sold. On the way, we passed Burgh House, which Peter told us was one of the oldest houses in Hampstead.

"I asked Sian to do that one," said Luke, "so we don't have to go in. Let's go and get a drink instead. I think we've earned one."

After the tour, we went and sat outside the Coffee Cup café in the village and chatted about what we'd learned and what we might put in our presentation. It was then I started to feel uncomfortable. Walking round with Luke had been okay, but sitting opposite him and looking straight into his eyes and he into mine, I felt strange, like my brain was going to fuse, and I was sure I was blushing madly. I didn't want to be feeling what I was feeling, and the more I tried to push the sensations to the back of my head, the more they seemed to want to be in the front. In the end I didn't look at him. Instead I watched the passersby as Luke continued talking and World War III started in my head.

You're in danger of becoming like Sian, said one voice at the back of my mind, and you know what Luke thinks of her. A mixed-up kid. Someone with a sad crush on him. You'll be another on a long list.

But he is very attractive, said another voice. Not

only looking, but personality-wise, as well. There's nothing wrong in appreciating beauty. It would be mad not too. Chill.

And on the voices went:

But he's Nesta's boyfriend.

So? You're not planning to steal him or anything.

No. I'm not. But I shouldn't flirt, either.

Don't kid yourself that he'd flirt with you. Someone like Luke would never look twice at someone like you, not in a fancying kind of way.

But I think he does like me.

So? There's a difference between liking someone and fancying them.

Erk! How many people are there inside my head?

"Are you listening to me, T. J.?" asked Luke. "You look like you're miles away. What are you thinking about?"

"Oh! Nothing. Er. Sorry," I said, getting up. "Look. Better go. Just realized the time."

He looked disappointed. "Sorry," he said. "I've been boring you, haven't I? Was I going on?"

"No, no . . . I just have to go."

Luke didn't look convinced. "Okay. See you Tuesday then, and we'll compare notes."

I started to head off.

"Hey, sure you don't want a lift?" Luke called after me.

"Nope. Thanks. Got to run," I said over my

shoulder, then hurried on. I must be mad, I thought. A lift would have been brilliant. Now I have to make my own way home. But I needed time on my own to think. Blow away the madness that seemed to be taking me over.

Okay, I told myself as I made my way home. Okay, so Luke is class A, five-star attractive. So is Orlando Bloom. Fine. I can appreciate them. It's fine. That's okay. Only looking. It would be insane not to acknowledge beauty and appreciate that someone is nice and interesting. Yeah. Madness not to. So no big deal. No problem. Maybe I'm getting a bug. Yeah. That's it. Probably a virus going round making me feel funny. Being out in the cold with all those strangers. Lot of bugs going round at this time of year. Flu, colds, fevers. Nothing more than that.

By the time I reached home, I felt calmer. More rational.

Got a bug. Sorted. Yes. No prob.

Some of the Famous People Who've Lived in Hampstead

Kingsley Amis, writer

W. H. Auden, poet

William Blake, artist

Richard Burton, actor

Agatha Christie, writer

John Constable, artist

Dame Judi Dench, actress

Charles Dickens, writer

Daphne Du Maurier, writer

George Du Maurier, cartoonist and novelist

Sigmund Freud, psychoanalyst

Thomas Hardy, writer

William Hogarth, artist

Aldous Huxley, writer

John Keats, poet

D. H. Lawrence, writer

A. A. Milne, writer

Florence Nightingale, nursing reformer

George Orwell, writer

George Romney, artist

Dante Gabriel Rossetti, artist and poet

Peter Sellers, actor

Sting (Gordon Sumner), musician

H. G. Wells, writer

Chapter 7

Worst Person in the World

We were in the graveyard at the back of the church on Church Row. It was snowing and everywhere looked white and magical.

"You're freezing," said Luke as he took off his red woolen scarf and wound it round my neck. Then he took the ends of the scarf and pulled me toward him. I could feel the warmth of his body through his coat. He reached up with his left hand and stroked the side of my cheek gently, then slid his hand down to my chin and tilted my face up to meet his. I looked into his eyes as his face moved toward mine, and our lips . . .

"ARRRRGGHHHHHHHHHHHHHHHHH!"

I sat up in a cold sweat. Where was I? Oh. Home.

Bed. Warm. I lay back down and pulled the duvet up to my neck. Omigod. I dreamed I was snogging Luke. Omigod. Sorted, huh? Got it all under control? Got some kind of a bug? Yeah, right. I might have my conscious mind under control, but my unconscious clearly had ideas of its own. And those ideas were getting up close and very personal with Nesta's boyfriend. I am clearly the worst person on the planet.

At school later, I felt even worse. Nesta was so nice to me, but then why shouldn't she be? She didn't know that I was having X-rated kisses with her boyfriend in my dreams.

"Luke said you had a good time on the walk," she said at breaktime as we made our way down toward the hall.

"Yeah. We did. There was so much to take in. We've got a ton of work to do. I knew there were a few famous people who lived in the area, but nothing like the number we've discovered."

Nesta put her arm through mine. "Luke thinks you don't like him," she said.

"*Whadt?* Why? What on earth gave him that impression?"

"Dunno." She shrugged. "I guess you can be cool with people sometimes. A bit aloof sort of thing."

"No. It's not that. I'm . . . I'm shy. . . ." Actually I'd heard people say that I was aloof before, but I never mean to be. It's when I don't know people very well, I go quiet. But I didn't think I had been with Luke. I thought we'd got on great. Too great.

"Is that what he said. I was aloof?"

Nesta nodded. "Something about you running off as soon as the walk was over, like you didn't want to hang out with him more than was necessary. He said that you're a bit of a mystery and don't give anything away. He was asking a lot about you."

Izzie raised an eyebrow. "Maybe he fancies her. Watch out, Nesta. You've got competition."

Nesta laughed so I joined in, probably a little too hysterically.

"Numpf. Er . . . as if . . . ," I said.

"I do think he rates you though, T. J. He said he thought you were really smart. I told him you were. The smartest person I know."

"Neeyuh, thanks." I felt lost for words. And a little hurt. He rates me because I'm smart. But he dates Nesta because she's beautiful.

Nesta put her hand on my arm. "T. J., for me, be nice to Luke. I mean, me, Iz, and Lucy know that you're a fabster, but when people don't know you, they might be intimidated by your distant cool manner. Maybe make a bit more of an effort to be friendly?"

I gulped. Me, distant? Cool? Hah! If only she knew the turmoil that went on in my head sometimes. And wanting me to be more *friendly* to Luke, she clearly didn't have the slightest idea what she was asking. And amazing! Luke thought I didn't *like* him. I thought it was written all over my face that I did.

"I think it's because you're cool that Steve likes you," said Lucy. "He said that you're not like other teenage girls, who shriek instead of talk and are always getting hysterical."

"Did he?" I asked. It's strange how other people see you and how you see yourself, I thought. This person they were describing didn't sound like me one bit. Cool? Aloof? Distant? More like totally mental. Mental girl from Mental Land, that's me.

"Steve said he's going to help you," said Lucy, linking my other arm. "Take photos."

"Um, yeah," I mumbled. Oh God. Steve. I felt like I'd betrayed him. I ought to have been dreaming about kissing him, not Luke. For a moment, I had a real ache to talk to Hannah. We'd been friends for so many years and talked over *everything*. She'd know what to say. How to play it. I looked at Lucy, Izzie, and Nesta. I'd *thought* I could talk to them about everything, but no way could I mention this. They'd hate me forever and think I was the worst person in the world, and maybe I was. Like, hey, guys, guess what I dreamed last night. I was snogging Luke and I think I fancy him. It's an unspoken rule: Thou shalt keep thy hands off other people's boyfriends.

After school Nesta and Lucy were going up to Highgate to meet Luke and Tony, and they asked if I wanted to join them and bring Steve. No *way*, I thought. Too many highly intuitive people in one small space. Despite my apparent cool demeanor, one of them would be bound to suss out what was going on in my head, so I made my excuses and headed for home.

Got to keep busy, I thought once I was on the bus. Stay out of Luke's way. Never be alone with him again. Be nice to him in company to keep Nesta happy. Then it will all be fine.

I spent the evening compiling a list of the famous people that lived in Hampstead, then I pulled out the photocopy of the map of the area that I'd done earlier at school and spent the evening putting stars on the map to show where they all lived. Luke will like this, I thought as I surveyed my work. It looked really good. Names of people, what they did, and the dates they lived in Hampstead on one side. The map with the stars showing where they lived in the middle, then the names and addresses on the right-hand side. It would look great when it was blown up. On a board next to it, I'd put the photographs of the houses where some of them lived that Steve was going to take for me. Yeah, it would look cool. Yeah. Cool. Like me. Not.

Outbox (1)
From: babewithbrains@psnet.co.uk
To: hannahnutter@fastmail.com
Date: 1 December
Subject: Boys. Urgent.

Dear Hannah,

Please reply to this as soon as you get it. No. Actually please read it first then reply. Haha.

Actually, not funny. Nothing funny about my situation. I think I may be the worst person in the world. I fancy Nesta's boyfriend, Luke. I dreamed I was snogging him last night, and now I feel really bad. And Nesta's being really sweet and telling me to make an effort to be more friendly to him. More friendly?!!!!

What shall I do? Shall I quit the project? I wish you were here really badly.

E-mail back soon.

Luv,
T. J.

P.S.: By the way, do you think that I'm aloof or distant?

From: <u>hannahnutter@fastmail.com</u>
To: <u>babewithbrains@psnet.co.uk</u>
Date: 2 December
Subject: Boys urgent

Ma petite little T. J.,

Chill. I fancy loads of my mates' boyfriends. Everybody does. What's the big deal? It's totally normal especially if they are cute, babe-type boyfriends. What are you supposed to do, cast out your eyes or something madly biblical? It's sooooo typical of you to get in a tizz over something like this, and it's because you are a nice person with a conscience. So you dreamed about him? Doesn't mean you snogged him in real life. So my advice is chill. Chill like a chilled thing. Don't quit the project. Why don't you tell Nesta? It's always nice to hear that a mate rates your boyfriend, and I bet you'll have a laugh about it.

Lots of love and I miss you too,
Hannah
P.S.: No, I don't think you're aloof, but I know other people at school, when I was there, were sometimes intimidated as you're such a mega brain. And you can be shy sometimes, so maybe people who don't know you take it as indifference or think that you're bored 'cause you don't say anything. Stuff 'em, I say. As the song goes: "Don't go changin' . . ."

E-mail: **Outbox (1)**
From: babewithbrains@psnet.co.uk
To: hannahnutter@fastmail.com
Date: 2 December
Subject: Guys. Urgent.

No way can I tell Nesta. Much as I love her, she has a big mouth. If I tell her I fancy Luke, yeah, we'll probably have a laugh, then she'll tell Izzie and Lucy. And Luke. They've already been talking about me. And if she told him, then I'd be too embarrassed to work on the project with him. So no way. But I will try and chill.

Chill. Chilling. Chilled.

Yours, the Ice Queen of Norf London. Gawd it's cold over here. And not just cuz I'm chilled. 'Tis 'cause 'tis winter.

Chapter 8

Skiving

By Wednesday evening I felt like I'd got myself together again. I'd be professional, competent, and detached. I'd be that person that people saw. Distant, cool. I could do it and not let any silly feelings get in the way.

Luke, Sian, and Olivia were already in the prefab when I got to the project meeting, and we launched into all our findings straight away. Sian had obviously been doing her homework, and she showed us the brochures that she'd picked up over the weekend.

"And there's another guided walk," she said looking at Luke hopefully, "only this time it's round Highgate. Sunday afternoon at 1:45."

"Excellent," said Luke. "Can you do it?"

Sian nodded.

"Okay, you and Olivia do that," he continued. "There really is a lot of ground to cover, so I reckon it's best if you two cover Highgate, and T. J. and I will focus on Hampstead."

"Oh, I don't mind doing Highgate," I said, "if Sian wants to do Hampstead with you."

Luke shook his head and looked at my lists and maps. "After this great start you've made? No way. In fact, T. J., I'd like to go down right now and look at D. H. Lawrence's house in the Vale of Health, if that's okay with you."

"Um, sure."

"Okay. Sian, Olivia. You hold the fort here, and T. J. and I will nip down there. There's plenty for you to do. Sort out which places you want to highlight in Highgate."

"Yes, sir," said Olivia with a mock salute.

Sian nodded but didn't look very happy. "But I wanted to go over what angle to take," she said indicating all her findings.

"We will," said Luke as he put on his coat. "I'll give you a call, and we'll get together. Okay?"

This time when she nodded, she looked happier.

"In fact," said Luke, "let's step things up a bit. Meet here again tomorrow night?"

"Yeah," said Sian. "Great."

"On second thought," Luke continued, "we should meet as many times as we need this week until we've got things really sorted. We need to get on top of this, put our other homework on the back burner until we know exactly what we're going to present, then we can kick back and relax a bit."

I think Sian thought he meant meetings just with her and looked delighted, but then Luke turned to Olivia. "You in?"

Olivia nodded.

"T. J.?"

"I'll do my best."

Poor Sian. Her face had fallen again. It looked like she was never going to get Luke on his own.

We drove down to the Vale of Health, and Luke parked the car at the top of the lane. It's a remarkable place, just off East Heath Road, and a lot of locals don't even know that it exists. It's like a countryside village hidden away at the bottom of Hampstead Heath.

We soon found the house where D. H. Lawrence lived as there was the typical blue plaque mounted on the outside wall.

"I didn't realize it was privately owned," said Luke with disappointment as he looked at the terraced house. From the bike in the front garden and computer at an upstairs window, it was clearly inhabited.

"Me neither," I said. "I thought it would be like the one at Keats Grove where it's a shrine to Keats. Ah well, never mind. I'll get Steve to photograph it anyway."

"I guess we could go and check out Keats House," sighed Luke, then he grinned and checked his watch, "*or* we could go and have a skive."

"Skive, like how?"

"Movie."

My first instinct was to say no, but then I remembered what Nesta had said about being more friendly.

"Yeah, sure. Where?"

"Ever been to the Everyman cinema in Hampstead village?"

I shook my head. "I've walked past a few times, but never been in. We always go to the one up near Finchley."

"Then you're in for a treat. And it's on me. I got some good tips last week working in Dad's restaurant."

"This is awesome," I said as an usherette showed us to our seats twenty minutes later.

Luke looked really pleased. "I know."

He'd paid top price so that we could sit upstairs in the private balcony, where there were a small number of plush leather chairs and sofas.

"Sit where you like," said the usherette. "It's quiet today."

"So where would madam like to sit?" asked Luke after she'd gone.

I sprawled in an enormous chair at the back. "Everywhere looks great," I said.

"This is my favorite," said Luke as he sat on a sofa on the second and back row.

I went and sat beside him. It was amazing. Totally luxurious and it felt like we were the only people in the cinema having a private viewing. A few minutes later, the lights went down and the trailers started up. Luke curled up happily in his corner of the sofa.

"Cool, huh?" he said.

"Major." I nodded back.

As the movie started, I found it hard to concentrate. I was so aware of Luke's proximity. At one point he sat up, and our knees were touching and just the pressure of his leg against mine was enough to send my head spinning. I moved my leg away then, a few minutes later our arms touched, and it felt like heat from him was burning into me. Then Luke slipped his shoes off and stretched out. "Sit back," he whispered. "Make the most of it."

I did as I was told, and he put his feet up and over my knees and grinned at me. "Heaven, huh?"

"Unuh . . . ," I whispered back. "H–Heaven."

Well, Nesta, I thought as I glanced down at Luke curled up comfortably like a cat, at least I'm doing as you told me. You can't get more friendly than this!

After the movie, Luke suggested we have a cappuccino in the bar downstairs. Once again my first instinct was to say no, but I'd run off last time we'd had coffee, and I didn't want him reporting back to Nesta again. And I remembered what Hannah had written. Chill. Everyone fancies their mate's boyfriend, especially if they're cute, babe types. Well, Luke was definitely that. And we did get along and have loads in common. I decided to chill and enjoy the moment. There was nothing wrong with that.

As Luke went to the bar, I sat in one of the armchairs and looked around. Fab, I thought, I really like it here. The atmosphere was a mixture of sophisticated and bohemian, with low lighting, dark walls, and velvet sofas and chairs, and there were framed black-and-white photos from old Bollywood films on the wall. I felt very grown-up sitting there with the other people sipping their wine and picking at bowls of olives.

"Very posh," I whispered to Luke, when he came back with the drinks. "I see they do olives here, not your common old popcorn."

A couple of teen girls came in and eyed Luke up, then looked enviously at me. I couldn't help but feel great to be the one that was with him.

As on the walk, Luke was interesting company, and we chatted about films we liked and ones we wanted to see. Just as I was starting to relax and enjoy myself, Luke went quiet for a few moments then looked at me intensely. No one had ever looked at me like that before, like he was really looking into me. I felt myself getting pinker and pinker.

"It's easy being with you, T. J. Watts," he said finally. "I wonder what would have happened if I'd met you before Nesta."

"Uh . . . nyah . . ."

That was me gone. I mean, what was I supposed to say? He'd completely thrown me. "Um, er . . . dunno, um. Like another coffee? No? Um. I would." And I was up and off to the counter before he could say anything else to blow my mind.

When I returned, Luke didn't press me for an answer. He glanced at his watch as I bolted back scalding coffee then he began looking at me again. My heart started to palpitate madly in my chest.

"Better get going I guess," I said, and stood up.

Like at the Coffee Cup café on Sunday, he looked disappointed, but he didn't object. "Sure," he said as he got up and put on his coat. "Yeah. I'll drop you off."

As we made our way back to the car, the traffic was busy and, for a brief moment as we crossed the road, he took my hand. I ran with him toward the pavement on the opposite side of the road. When I glanced to my left, I noticed that someone had stopped and was staring at us. It was Lal. Lal, as in Steve and Lucy's brother Lal. And he had a very quizzical look on his face. Then he turned on his heel and stomped off round a corner.

E-mail: **Outbox (1)**
From: babewithbrains@psnet.co.uk
To: hannahnutter@fastmail.com
Date: 3 December
Subject: Heeeeeeelp!!!!!

Dear Hannah,

Oh God am I in trouble Nesta told me to be more friendly so I was and when Luke suggested a skive to the movies I went and he took my hand when we crossed the road and Lal Lovering saw us and Luke asked me what I thought would have happened if he'd met me before he'd met Nesta oh God, what did he mean? Maybe nothing and he took my hand (the second time by the way) does that mean anything? Maybe not as he is Italian and I think he's a naturally touchy-feely type person maybe I'm imagining things oh God Hannah, come back to England all is forgiven I have no one to talk to over here and it's driving me mad. I'm beginning to think that a move to Devon might be best after all.

Tell me what to DOOOO! I neeeeeeeeeeeed you.

Love, your friend,
Mad Person

E-mail: **Inbox (1)**
From: hannahnutter@fastmail.com
To: babewithbrains@psnet.co.uk
Date: 4 December
Subject: Heeellppp

Hohohahaha. My little percorini. What a merry old state you is in back there in Britland. First thing. Breathe. Second thing. Breathe again.

Sounds like this guy Luke is flirting with you. He's checking you out for definite. Yes, the holding hand thing may be innocent, but I don't think the question was. Think about it. Would you have ever in your wildest dreams have asked him what he thought would have happened if you'd met him before you met Steve? No. Exactly. Comprendi? This guy sounds like trouble. Be mucho, mucho careful.

Try to avoid situations where you're alone with him. And don't give anything away 'cause then he's gotcha.

Still sweltering here. Don't fancy anyone big time at the mo, which is quite nice as there's a group of us that just hang out.

Luv and kisses,
Auntie Hannah

Chapter 9

Week From
Hell

"Lucy phoned," said Mum as soon as I walked though the door after the movie with Luke.

"When?"

"About five minutes ago."

"Did she leave a message?"

"Only to phone her as soon as you get back."

"How did she sound?"

"What do you mean? Like Lucy. Why? Is something going on?"

"No."

I raced up the stairs and stared at the phone. How was I going to get out of this? Mojo was scrabbling outside my door, so I let him in, and he jumped on the end of my bed, where he lay wagging his tail.

"God, I so wish you could talk, Mojo," I said as he rolled over and I tickled his tummy. "Come on, talk to me. What's on the top of a house? Come on . . ."

"Rufff," barked Mojo.

"That's right! A roof. And how am I feeling?"

"Rurrf," he replied. "Rfff, rrfff."

"Right again, I *am* feeling rough," I said. Mojo looked so pleased with himself that he rolled back on his legs, sprang up, and gave my face a huge lick. "See, you can talk if you try," I told him.

By the eager expression on Mojo's face, he was doing his best, but I decided to ask someone who spoke proper English instead. I e-mailed Hannah, then lay back on my bed and stared at the ceiling. Two minutes later, the phone rang again. I let it ring and didn't pick up my extension.

"T. J., it's for you," Mum called up the stairs. "Lucy."

I took a deep breath and picked up the phone.

"Hey, Lucy," I said in my most cheerful voice.

"So what's going on?" asked Lucy.

Lal obviously hadn't wasted any time reporting back.

"Oh, same old same old," I replied, trying to avoid the tone in her voice. I knew exactly what she meant by "going on."

"You and Luke," said Lucy. "Lal said he saw you."

"Oh *that*."

"Yeah, that. Lal said you and Luke were holding hands."

"Not really."

"Well, you either were or you weren't."

"We were, but not as in holding hands holding hands if you know what I mean. He took my hand when we crossed the road, that's all. Traffic safety. He was probably a boy scout trained to steer old-age pensioners across. Nothing's going on. Lucy, you know I'd never . . ."

"Do you fancy him?"

"*Noooo*. No way. Course not. I mean, yeah, he's really attractive, but he's not my type. And anyway, Lucy, you know I'd never do that to Nesta. Or Steve. Hey, Lucy come on, you guys are my friends."

"Well, okay. Just checking, because I know Steve would be gutted and so would Nesta if you were carrying on with Luke."

I felt near to tears. I really wanted to tell her everything, but I didn't dare in case it came out wrong and made things worse than they were. "But I'm *not*. Honestly. Lucy, you've *got* to believe me."

"So where had you been?"

"Movie. Luke wanted to skive, and I was going to say I couldn't go, but Nesta *told* me to be more friendly to him. Remember? You were there. You heard her. I would never, ever, *ever* take anyone else's boyfriend. Especially Nesta's. You've *got* to believe me."

There was a pause for a few seconds. "I do. Sorry. It's probably just Lal, you know what he's like, he came in all flustered about what he'd seen. You know what a crush he has on Nesta. He was probably hoping you were going to run off with Luke, then he could step in and comfort Nesta. Sorry. I should have known it was innocent."

After she'd put the phone down, I lay back on the bed. That's done it, I thought. I've lied to one of my best friends. It was true that I wouldn't be disloyal to Nesta and nothing was *really* going on. It was in my head though. And I did fancy Luke. Like crazy. Oh, hell. What a week. The week from hell. And it was only Wednesday.

At school on Thursday, Lucy was fine, her usual sunny self, and Nesta didn't mention the hand-holding episode, so I presumed that Lucy had thought it best to keep quiet about it. I felt relieved as our friendship carried on as normal. I only wished my head did. Try as I might, I couldn't stop thinking about Luke, over and over again, how he'd looked at me when he'd asked what might have happened if he'd met me before he'd met Nesta. How it felt when he kicked off his shoes in the cinema and put his legs over my knees like we were the oldest and easiest of friends. How it had felt when he'd taken my hand when we crossed the road. And I couldn't help but imagine what it would be like to kiss him. The thought of it made me tingle from my head to my toes. I tried to put him out of my mind, but he wouldn't go, and I couldn't help but look forward to the meeting after school and seeing him again.

However, at the project meeting later, it was clear that Luke wasn't feeling the same way. He blanked me—that is, he talked to me, told me what to do, but he didn't look at me. Not properly. Not once. It was as if he couldn't meet my eyes. I wondered if maybe he felt bad about last night and felt like he'd been disloyal to Nesta. I was disappointed on one level but, on another, I felt relieved. It made it easier to deal with, and once again I told myself to get over him and get a grip.

When I arrived at the meeting on Friday, Luke was already there, and he was totally opposite to how he was the day before. He looked right at me, then started complaining about his neck and asked me to give it a rub. At first I was going to refuse, but what excuse could I give? That I daren't touch him? He might have thought I was mad, or a sad case, like Sian with a pathetic schoolgirl crush on someone she can't have. Or maybe I should have come clean and said I felt a bit weird because of Nesta. But then he might have thought I was a prude. He'd only asked for a neck rub. It wasn't like he'd asked me to snog him. And if anyone else had asked for a neck rub, I wouldn't have thought it was any big deal. I'd just have done it. My anxiety soon faded as I started to massage him. It felt amazing just to touch his shoulders and his neck, and he sighed like he was enjoying it too. I know I wasn't imagining that the air grew charged, and at one point he put his hand up on top of mine and left it there for a few moments, then he leaned back against me, and we stayed like that for a while. Nothing said. I felt this strange feeling—a mixture of sadness and closeness as I knew we couldn't go any further than an innocent neck rub. I'm sure he was feeling the same, because he said this weird thing out of the blue. "Unspoken but not unknown," he said. And that was all. I knew what he meant. Only a neck rub, only a neck rub, I kept telling myself, but it felt like much more. But when we heard Sian and Olivia approaching, he leaped up quickly and started looking busy. He wouldn't have done that if it was innocent, would he? Maybe my feelings were not as one-sided as I thought. What the hell is going on? I asked myself for the hundredth time that week.

On Saturday, we were due to have another quick meeting in the morning, but I was late as my bus got held up in traffic. I peeked through the window before I went in, and this time when I arrived Sian was alone with Luke. I could hardly believe my eyes as she was massaging his neck. I felt sick at the thought that he'd asked another girl to do it for him and looked like he was enjoying it. Olivia arrived a few moments after me and saw me looking in the window. When she saw them together, she glanced at me and raised an eyebrow as if to say, What's going on here then? I wondered myself, and all through the meeting, my head was all over the place. Yesterday I'd thought that there was something special between Luke and me. Had I imagined it? Not from my side I hadn't. I had no doubt that I felt a lot for Luke, and although I had no intention of ever acting on it, I couldn't deny those feelings. It must happen to people all the time. You meet someone, you go out with them, then you meet someone else you fancy. Doesn't mean you leave your first boyfriend. But then, was it all in my head? Maybe I *was* just like Sian? Another girl on a long list of people who had a crush on Luke. I so wished I could talk to my mates about it all, especially Nesta. If it had been about any other boy, she'd have been brilliant to talk it over with, as boys are her speciality. But because it was Luke, her boyfriend, I reminded myself for the umpteenth time, I could never bring the subject up. I felt miserable and mixed-up. I didn't want to be feeling any of it, but every now and then, Luke would catch my eye in the meeting and not look away for a few seconds, and the look in his eyes was so tender. My stomach did backflips and somersaults. There was something there. There was. I *couldn't* be imagining it, could I? For a brief moment I felt like thumping him and yelling, "Don't *look* at me like that! Stop *playing* with my head!" But then he might have thought I was bonkers. And Sian and Olivia definitely would! One time Olivia noticed Luke and me looking at each other, and I looked away quickly. Got to get out of here quick, I told myself, but then another part wanted to stay and look into his eyes one more time.

After the meeting had ended, try as I might, I couldn't make myself walk away when Sian and Olivia left. I fussed about with my coat, shuffled my papers, packed and repacked my rucksack until finally Luke looked up.

"Did you want something?" asked Luke as he gathered up his things.

I felt uncomfortable. I should have gone. Left. Got the bus. I felt like I had the wrong body on. The wrong clothes. My head didn't fit the rest of me.

"Er . . . we need to talk . . . ," I started, then, as Luke rolled his eyes, I remembered that Nesta had told me that those were the four words that most boys dread. "Er, it's nothing really," I continued trying to make my voice light. "Um . . . how's your neck?"

Luke rotated his chin. "Better actually."

"Yeah, I noticed that you got Sian to give you a rub earlier." It was out before I could help it, and I knew my tone sounded jealous.

Luke stopped what he was doing, sighed heavily, and looked at me. "You're not going to go weird on me, are you?"

I felt my heart sink. "What do you mean?"

"Sian. Neck rub. It's all innocent, you know."

"Yeah. I know."

"Good. Because I credit you with more intelligence than reading things into things that aren't there."

"Yeah. Right." The atmosphere felt heavy, all wrong. I was doing a saddo. Needy. Hanging on where I wasn't wanted in the hope of another look, a word of encouragement, anything to let me know that I wasn't alone in what I was feeling.

Luke pulled his jacket on. "See you then."

"Yeah. See you."

Arrghhhhhh, I thought as I watched him walk off. Don't read things into things? Did he mean between me and him or between him and Sian? Hell. I was dying to ask him, but then I might make myself look a *real* fool. Desperate. Clingy. And I know how much boys hate that. And besides, there was Steve and Nesta to think of. Luke might be a totally innocent party, and if I blabbed out all my feelings, he might think I was the most crapola girlfriend in the world and the lousiest friend. Don't give anything away, Hannah had said.

I was losing my mind and desperately needed

someone to talk to. But who? Nesta was off the list because of Luke. Lucy was off the list because of Steve. Mojo was no good, and e-mailing Hannah wasn't enough anymore. She was too far away. I needed someone who knew everyone involved. Someone who could give me some good advice.

Forget looking a fool, I thought. You've got nothing to lose.

I decided to take a chance, got out my mobile, and dialed.

The four words boys most dread: We need to talk.

Chapter 10

Yogis

"So what's up, doc?" said Izzie with a smile as she let me into her house, then we made our way up the stairs to her bedroom.

"Oh, nothing," I said when we got to her room, and I flopped on to the bed.

"Want some lunch?"

I shook my head. "Not hungry."

Izzie sat at her desk. "You said you needed to talk to me. Sounded urgent."

"Yeah. No. I mean . . . just to catch up. How's it all going? You know, your side of the project?"

Izzie smiled mischievously. "Cool. In fact, I'm having a total gas with Trevor. He's slowly coming round to my way of thinking. I told him that no way could we concentrate only on the Christian development of the area. Now we're looking at all sorts of stuff. All the religions. The persecution of witches, mysticism, magic . . . he's getting into it. And I even persuaded him to have his hair cut into a decent style."

"You'll be persuading him to get a tattoo next," I said, laughing.

"Not a bad idea. But it's been good. We've discovered loads of interesting stuff, like, you know that place in Highgate, Pond Square?"

I nodded.

"Well, there aren't any ponds there anymore, but there used to be. Two of them. And one of them was used to duck women in. . . ."

"Witches?"

"No. Just women who nagged their husbands! I'm going to suggest that they bring the tradition back for parents who nag their children. My mum will be a regular."

I laughed. Izzie's relationship with her mother was tempestuous at the best of times. They were total opposites. Her mum was neat, organized, and mega straight. Izzie was into everything, curious, and open-minded. They often clashed when Izzie discovered some new fad, religion, or therapy and decided to change her life for the umpteenth time.

Izzie pulled her chair closer to the bed. "You

know if you *do* need to talk, T. J., I'm happy to listen and not just about project stuff."

"I know. I . . ." I *desperately* wanted to talk to her. Spill it all out. But there was still a part of me that was worried that she'd hate me. Izzie and Lucy went back a long way, mates in junior school and best mates ever since. And both had been friends with Nesta longer than I had. And then there was the fact that Steve was Lucy's brother, and she was very protective of him. I didn't want to get on the wrong side of Lucy, as the wrong side of her would include Izzie. But then again, Izzie was my friend too, and apart from all her mad ideas, she was good at giving advice. "God, it's so complicated . . . ," I began.

"Try me," said Izzie.

"It's nothing really, just . . . oh . . . I don't know. . . . I don't know where to begin. . . ."

"Something's obviously bothering you, and it's always better out than in."

I decided to trust her. I was going to crack up if I didn't. "If I tell you, promise you won't tell anyone else?"

"Promise."

"Okay. I . . . I just feel like I'm going totally mental. See, this thing happened recently, and I can't stop thinking about it, and I don't want to think about it, but I can't stop myself. And the more I try and stop myself, the more I think about it. . . ."

"Ah," said Izzie. "Thing. A boy."

I nodded. I knew she'd understand. "Not just any boy."

"Not Steve?"

I shook my head. "Not Steve."

"Ah. Who, then?"

"Er . . . um . . . er . . ." I looked at the carpet. "Luke."

"*Luke?* Oh!"

"I know. Oh."

"Has anything happened between you?"

"*No.* It can't. Won't. No. It's all in my stupid, stupid head."

"Well, he *is* a bit of a dish," said Izzie.

"Do you fancy him?" I asked.

"I think he's stunning, but no, the chemistry's not there, and no matter how gorgeous someone is, if the magic's not there, it's not there. And it ain't with us."

That got me thinking again. Chemistry. It was definitely there between Luke and me. Whenever we saw each other, he was like a magnet and I was an iron filing. I had no choice but to be drawn toward him. I couldn't help it. It was chemistry.

"It's . . . look, I know he's Nesta's boyfriend," I said, "and I respect that. I would never go after him. It's just . . . as you said, chemistry."

"Yeah, but you can feel chemistry with loads of people, even people you don't fancy or know it would never work with. I felt it with this complete dork on holiday a couple of years ago. He worked on the beach and was so full of himself, running about like he was some lifeguard stud when actually he had skinny legs, was lily-white pale, and his job was to collect money for the deckchairs. The chemistry was really strong, but no way would I have followed it through. It was weird. Feeling an attraction and a repulsion at the same time."

"I know. I *know*. And some people are out of bounds. I've been thinking about it a lot. Like when people get married. Doesn't mean they stop feeling attracted to other people, but they have made a vow to be faithful, so if they feel chemistry with someone else, most times, they let the chemistry go."

"Right," said Izzie. "But Luke and Nesta aren't married."

"But she is my mate. To me that means hands off her boyfriend. My mates mean a lot to me."

"Likewise," said Izzie.

"And my mates are mainly why I don't want to move to Devon. Or didn't. I don't know anymore. Now with this thing with Luke . . . maybe it would be for the best. . . ."

Izzie looked surprised. "That bad, huh? So. I take it that you've felt some vibe with Luke, then?"

"I think so. I mean, yes. Definitely, most definitely, but I'd never act on it. Honest. It's just difficult having to do the project with him and all. It's so *strong*. It's like I'm caught in a powerful current in a river, and it's carrying me along, but I know I can't go with it so I'm swimming the opposite way. It's wearing me *out*."

"Hmm," said Izzie, then she grinned. "So get out of the river!"

"What? *How?*"

She turned to her desk, picked up a leaflet, and read from it. "'If you want uncomplicated love, follow me.'"

I waited for her to continue. Which she didn't.

"What's that supposed to mean?"

"Buddhism," she said. "I've been reading about it. See, there are many kinds of love, although we use the same word for all of them. We love our pets, we love our parents, we love our brothers and sisters, we love our friends, we *love* chocolate. All the same word, 'love,' but very different levels of it and each level has its own complications. We love some boys. That's the most complicated kind of love of all. It brings insecurity, jealousy, loss of focus, madness."

"Tell me about it." I thought about the range of emotions I'd been through over the last few days—excitement, insanity, highs, lows, tenderness, expectation, disappointment, sadness, elation, despair . . .

"Buddha says that the source of all unhappiness is desire," continued Izzie. "One desire always leads to another, which is why we're never content. We get one thing, we want another. We get a new top, great, hurrah. Next week, we don't like it anymore, and we see one we want even more, and on and on it goes, with us always thinking that getting these things will make us happy. But it doesn't. It makes us agitated. We fancy a boy. We want to hold his hand, we want to snog him and on it goes. . . ."

"Yeah. So? All that stuff's totally normal. How do you stop it?"

"By going beyond desire. Buddha calls it a wheel, always turning. What you have to do is go to the center of the wheel through meditation, and there you'll find peace and stillness."

She made it sound so simple. Then she got out one of her yoga books and showed me a meditation where I had to block my right nostril with my thumb and breathe in through the left nostril, then block the left nostril, with my middle finger and breathe out through the right one. Over and over. By the end of my visit, I did feel slightly calmer, mainly because I kept losing track of which nostril I was supposed to be breathing in or out of and which finger or thumb was where, so my mind was distracted from Luke for a brief time.

"We can be yogis," said Izzie.

"Mmm. Maybe. Not sure I've got the hang of this," I said.

She reassured me that practice makes perfect, so I

decided to give it a go. I was going to be a yogi, get out of the river, and find the center of the wheel. Or something like that.

Centered, peaceful, focused. Off the cycle of desire. I am free, I told myself as I went home. In one nostril, out the other. Then I wondered what you did if you had a cold and your nose was stuffed up. Was that the end of your inner calm?

On Sunday, all the gang arranged to meet up at Costa in Highgate for our usual Sunday morning natter. Lucy was there first with Tony. Then Izzie arrived with her nostrils. Soon after her, Nesta came in the door with Luke and, as soon as I saw them, I went into my meditation. Block one nostril, breathe in the other. . . .

"Do you need a tissue?" asked Lucy.

"No," I said. "I'm meditating."

"Then do it in private," laughed Lucy. "It looks like you're picking your nose."

"My most alluring look." I grinned back at her. Izzie smiled over at me. It was going to be okay.

As we caught up on the week and what we'd all been doing, I made sure that I didn't look directly at Luke. However, I couldn't help but notice how friendly he was with everyone. His hand on Izzie's arm as he enthused about the project, hand resting on Lucy's shoulder when he got up and asked if anyone wanted anything from the counter. Yes, he's definitely a touchy-feely kind of person, I thought. Him holding my hand the other day was just another example. It meant nothing. At least, not to him. A few more nostrilly-breathing things and I'd be fine. A blip. A minor setback. No biggie.

But then Nesta got up to help Luke fetch drinks, and when they were in the queue, they started fooling around and soon the whole café was witnessing an Oscar-winning snog. Nesta never was one to be shy about who was watching her. I tried to look away, but I couldn't. It was awful. I felt like someone had stabbed me with a knife. Jealousy. It can hurt like hell. It was so clear. Luke was totally into Nesta, and I had a sad schoolgirl crush on him. It was all in my head. And always would be. I was pathetic. Sad. Pitiful.

Then I noticed Lucy looking at me.

Then Izzie looked at Nesta and Luke, then back at me.

Then Lucy looked at Izzie looking at me.

Then Lucy looked at me. At Nesta and Luke. Back at Izzie. Then back at me.

I felt like a rabbit caught in the spotlight as both of them stared me. Izzie with concern. Lucy with questions.

Lucy knows, I thought. She *knows* that something is going on in my head. I tried my nostril breathing without the aid of my thumb, but it looked like I was holding back a sneeze. So much for me being a yogi, I thought, as I got up and headed for the ladies' room at the back of the café, where I kicked the wall and almost broke my toe. I can't go on with this, I thought. Everyone can see right through me, and any minute now Steve and Lal are going to get here as well. Lal who already suspects something is going on and Steve, who is like Lucy, as sharp as a knife and would suss me out in no time.

There was only one thing for it.

Yoga Meditation

1) Sit comfortably with the spine straight.

2) For this technique, you are going to inhale and exhale through alternate nostrils. First put your right hand up to your face. Lightly rest your right thumb on the right side of your nose.

3) Rest your index finger on your forehead and have your middle finger ready by the left nostril for when you need it. The hand fits quite comfortably into this position.

4) When you are ready, apply a slight pressure with the thumb, closing the right nasal passage.

5) Now slowly inhale through the left nostril, hold for two counts then apply gentle pressure on the left nostril with your middle finger (releasing your thumb from the right nostril as you do so) and exhale slowly through the right nostril.

6) Then, with the middle finger still resting on the left nostril, inhale through the right nostril, slowly, hold for two counts, then lift the middle finger from the left nostril and exhale through the left, closing the right nostril with your thumb again.

7) Try a few times to get the movements right, then do it slowly up to ten times. Once you have mastered the technique, you can sit and do it for ten minutes or longer and it will bring about a sensation of calm and focus (unless you're T. J.).

Chapter 11

Another
Level?

"Mum, I have something I want to say to you."

"You're back early, T. J.," said Mum, looking up from the chair where she was doing the *Telegraph* crossword. "I thought you were out with the girls."

"I was, but I've been thinking, and I wanted to tell you something straight away."

"What is it?"

"About Devon. I've changed my mind. I want to go."

Mum smiled and put her paper aside. "I thought you might come round in the end, but . . ."

"When are we going?"

"But what's brought on this sudden change?"

"Nothing. Be good to have a new start. Er, I want to be a writer. New experience, fresh fields, et cetera. That sort of thing. So. When are we going?"

"Oh, T. J. There's so much to sort out, and we've only just started thinking about it. We haven't even put the house on the market yet, and there's so much your dad has to sort out with his position at the hospital."

"Okay. So, how about I go and live with Marie in the meantime? Get used to my new school."

Mum took off her reading glasses and peered at me. "T. J., what's going on? Sit down for a moment. Has something happened?"

I hovered behind the chair by the fireplace. "No. Why do you always have to think something's happened? I've simply changed my mind, and now I think that Devon is a great idea. The sooner the better. So. Shall I call Marie?"

"No. You won't call Marie. She's got enough on her plate at the moment, what with starting her new job and wedding plans. Something's going on. What is it, T. J.?"

"*Nothing.* Honestly," I replied as I headed out of the sitting room. "I'd tell you if there was."

Mum looked like she believed every word of it. Not. But what would I say to her? I've got a crush on one of my best friends' boyfriend, and I'm going slowly mental. What would she say? What could anyone say, except, Get over it, saddo.

Must rethink the plan, I thought as I lay on my bed ten minutes later and stared at the ceiling as if I was going to find the answer magically written there. Must rethink the plan. My mind had gone into overdrive. What was I going to do? I couldn't face school if they all knew. What if Izzie had told Lucy what I'd told her. And she'd told Nesta. And Nesta had told Steve and Luke. And . . . oh God oh God oh God. . . .

A moment later, I heard the phone ring. Oh no, I thought as I put a pillow over my head. It's probably one of the girls, and I'm to be hauled in front of the judge and jury. It wasn't me guv, honest, I'm innocent.

"T. J.," called Mum. "Phone for you. It's Luke."

Luke? What on earth does he want? I wondered as I reached for the extension. Oh please, God, Jesus, Buddha, Krishna, in fact anybody who's up there and might be listening, please don't let anyone have told Luke that I fancy him.

"Hey, Watts," he said. "What you doing?"

"Not much," I said. Going totally bonkers would be the correct answer, but I wasn't going to tell him that.

"How about we go and check out Keats' House in South Hampstead?" he asked. "It's open this afternoon."

He sounded cool enough. Maybe it was okay, and no one had said anything. "I thought you were doing something with Nesta," I said.

"Yeah, I was, then Lucy was in a panic about the

project and asked Nesta if she could give her a hand. So, she went off with her. So how about Keats' House?"

"Sorry. Can't."

"I thought you said you weren't doing much.'

"Er . . . got homework, you know. . . ."

The tone of Luke's voice suddenly changed from cheery to more serious. "Please, T. J. I . . . I . . . look, I think I . . . you were right the other day. We *do* need to talk. Meet me in half an hour?"

Need to talk? Oh hell. Someone *has* said something.

"What about?"

"Not on the phone. Please come."

He sounded so serious that my curiosity got the better of me, and I agreed to go. As I quickly got ready and headed out, my mind was spinning. Needed to talk? What about? The project? Somehow I doubted it. Maybe Sian again? What?

As I made my way down the front path, I noticed that Mum was watching me through the window.

"Bye, back later," I mouthed, and gave her a wave. Her expression looked concerned. I hoped that she wasn't going to do an inquisition later. There was nothing I could tell any of them. I didn't know what was going on myself.

Luke was waiting for me outside the bookshop in South End Green. He looked up and smiled when he saw me and my heart missed a beat.

"Hey," he said. "Thanks for coming. Grab a hot chocolate before we go?"

"Sure," I said. "Yes. Chocolate. Good."

Luke led us toward the café, where he took a quick look inside. "Bit crowded in there. Shall we sit outside? More private?"

I nodded. *Private?* My earlier instinct that he didn't just want to talk about the project had been right. Eek. It was freezing outside, but if he wanted privacy, then I wasn't going to argue, and with a bit of luck, the cold weather might stop me from blushing every time he looked at me. As he went inside to get drinks, my brain went into overdrive again. What on earth would he need to talk to me about that he didn't want anyone to overhear?

He came back a few minutes later and we sat in silence. I sensed that whatever it was he wanted to say, he wasn't finding it easy, and I tried to give him a reassuring smile. I could listen. I could be like Izzie. Maybe I should tell him about Buddhism and the nostril-breathing thingy. Then again, maybe not. Izzie can get away with New Age self-help advice. Not me. He'd think I was mad. The waitress brought us two big mugs of hot chocolate, and we sat and drank them for a while, once again in silence. Funny thing silence, I thought. It can be comfortable, uncomfortable, peaceful, tense, long and drawn out, concentrated, dreamy, amicable. This one felt awkward.

In the end, I couldn't stand it any longer. "So what did you want to talk about?"

Luke looked at the pavement, then into the café, then over the road at the trees. "Nesta," he said after a few moments.

"Nesta?"

Luke nodded. "Nesta."

So far, it's a riveting conversation, I thought. He says a name, I repeat it back.

"Has she said something?" I asked as paranoia took grip, and I tried to mentally prepare myself for Izzie having spilled the beans.

Luke looked confused. "Said something? Like what?"

"I don't know. Um. Let's rewind the tape a few moments. So. Nesta?"

"Yes, Nesta. I need to talk about what to do next."

Oh *no,* I thought. He's going to ask me for advice about Nesta. I should have known. I'm her mate, he probably wants some inside information. Lucy once told me that it happened all the time with boys and Nesta. They were always approaching Lucy to ask how to get off with her or get a date or something. But then Luke was already dating her, so what could he want from me?

"Okay," I said. "What to do next. In what sense?"

Luke sighed and looked back at the pavement. "It's not working out."

Not working out? *Noooooooo*. That's not part of the script. Not the one in my head anyway.

"I mean, she's really great," Luke continued, "it's just . . . I'm not sure I want to be as involved as she does. It all happened pretty fast and . . . oh, I don't know. . . ."

I don't know either, I thought. Why tell me? What does he want from me? How to tell her? How to break the bad news?

"I . . . er . . . does she have any idea?" I asked.

Luke finally looked at me and as always my stomach did a somersault. "No. No idea, I think. And I don't want to hurt her. I like her. She's great." He smiled. "High maintenance, but great. With you, it's much easier. . . ."

"What do you mean? High maintenance?"

"Oh, you know Nesta. She's a star, and stars need to be the center of attention all the time. And she wants me full-time, and I'm not sure that I want the same thing, at least not with her anyway. I know most blokes would think I was mad. She's stunning, but in the end, well, there's got to be something else, hasn't there? Chemistry."

"But I thought you did have . . . chemistry," I said, thinking about the Hollywood snog they'd done earlier in the queue at the café and everything Nesta had said about them being in love.

"So did I. But then I . . . it's like at school. There's

chemistry and then there's advanced chemistry, if you know what I mean." At this point he gave me a searching look. "I can talk to you. It's easier with you. Well, in one way it is; in another, it's more complicated. Steve. Nesta. I don't want to hurt anyone, but . . ." He reached over and took my hand and stroked the back of it gently with his thumb. I pulled it back.

"Don't."

Luke looked hurt. "Why not?"

"Because . . . I . . ." I wasn't exactly clear what he was saying about Nesta. Or me. It's hard breaking up with someone, and he might just need a hand to hold, I quickly told myself. Even so, I couldn't handle the effect it was having on me. I couldn't sit there holding hands, comforting him because things weren't working out with Nesta. Even if he was going to finish with her. It felt disloyal.

"Because you what?" Luke asked, and reached for my hand again.

It was too much for me, and I pulled my hand back once more. "Because I can't handle it," I blurted. "You might only be holding my hand but . . . to me . . . I can't help but . . . I . . ."

Luke put both of his hands over mine and held on to them so that I couldn't pull away. "I think you know it's not just me holding your hand."

"But you hold *everyone's* hand. I've seen you, arm

round this person, having a massage from that . . ."

"Oh, you mean Sian? I told you, there's nothing there. Not like with us. I think you know that what we have is on another level."

Don't give anything away, said Hannah's voice at the back of my head. I was longing to ask him what he meant, "on another level"? Did he mean a special friendship? Platonic? What kind of level? Chill, I told myself. Don't make a fool of yourself. He wants advice as to how to finish with Nesta and thinks that he can talk to me. One of the lads, that's me. Scott next door used to tell me that he liked me for that reason, because I was nonthreatening. One of the boys. Not fanciable, that's what he meant. That's a level of sorts. Luke wants advice, and I'm easy to talk to. That's all. Don't read anything into it, I told myself. He's clearly upset about having to finish with Nesta and that's why he's holding my hand. I mustn't, *mustn't* give anything away about the madness in my own mind. It's the last thing he needs on top of everything else at this moment in time.

I put my "one of the boys" hat on. "Luke, I think you ought to be talking to Nesta about this, not me. I'm sorry, but she's one of my best friends, and I feel disloyal. I can't tell you what to do or say, and I can't be a go-between. I know it's hard, but if it's not working out then you have to tell her. Let her know before anyone else. It's only fair on her."

Luke let go of my hand, drained his cup, nodded then looked at me sadly. "Yes, of course. I understand," he said. "Of course."

He stood up and gave himself a shake as if shaking off his mood. "Okay, Watts," he said in a more cheerful voice. "Let's go check out Keats's place. Apparently he was in love with some woman who lived there called Fanny Brawne." He laughed. "All these people pining for people they can't have. Round and round we go. Tough old life, isn't it?"

And off he went in the direction of Keats' Grove. Phew, I thought as I followed him. I think that was okay. I think that was the right thing to do, to say. But poor Nesta. She's not going to be happy about this, not one bit. I'll have to do everything I can to help and see her through it.

As we walked around Keats' House, Luke reverted to his usual self, talking about the project, and it was easy to respond to him on that level. I told him what I'd read about the poets from Keats's era, and he seemed impressed. He didn't mention Nesta again. My mind, however, couldn't let go so easily and kept replaying and replaying the things he'd said, the way he'd looked at me, how it had felt when he stroked my hand. What had he meant? People pining for people they can't have? Keats? Sian? Nesta? Or *me*? Could he have meant me? And what did he mean by saying that what we had was on another level?

Good-friends level? Bonded-over-our-shared-interest-in-history level? We-can-talk-to-each-other-easily level? Or what? Don't go there, I told myself. Don't go into "Or what?" If by any miraculous chance Luke did feel the same way about me as I felt about him, then this time was even worse than before. No one must ever know. To fancy Luke when he was going out with Nesta was one thing, but to act on it even in the slightest way when he was about to break up with her would be even worse. She's going to hurt enough without one of her best friends doing the dirty on her. No, I thought as Luke bent over a display to read an ancient book, then beckoned me over to read what it said. It can never happen. Never. Never. Never.

Quote From a Letter John Keats wrote to Fanny Brawne:

"I love you too much to venture into Hampstead. I feel it is not paying a visit but venturing into a fire."

Chapter 12

Unrequited
Twins

I was dreading the next project meeting on Wednesday and in the meantime watched Nesta closely for clues that Luke might have said something to her. Clearly not by the way she behaved and talked, as though everything was normal. Lucy on the other hand seemed concerned about my relationship with Steve.

"He really missed you when you dashed off on Sunday," she said at break on Monday.

"Yeah, sorry, I wasn't feeling too good," I blustered. "Got a bit of a bug."

"I thought you didn't seem your usual self, didn't I, Izzie? Remember I said to you."

Izzie raised an eyebrow but didn't say anything.

"Are you okay now? Are you cooling off toward Steve?" asked Lucy. "He says you haven't been around much lately."

I shook my head. "Been busy. There's so much to do on the project and so little time."

Unseen by Lucy, Izzie raised her other eyebrow. Was this a new type of meditation? Eyebrows now instead of nostrils or was she trying to say something? You never knew with Izzie.

Lucy nodded. "Yeah, I know what you mean. It has been full on. But you will tell Steve if you're going off him, won't you? I'd hate to see him hurt, and I want to be prepared for any reactions."

"Yeah. Course. But my feelings for him haven't changed. Honest," I said. It was true. They hadn't changed. I still really liked Steve, always would, but I couldn't deny that what I felt for Luke was on another level. Oh, hell. There's that expression again. Did Luke mean what I mean by another level? As in fancy-like-mad, never-felt-this-way-before-in-my-life type level? Oh, shut up, shut up, shut up, I told myself as we went into math.

By the time Wednesday came round, I was feeling marginally saner. Everything was okay with the girls; clearly nobody had said anything, and I had it clear in my mind that if I could just get through the project and see Nesta through the breakup with Luke, then I wouldn't have to see him again. It would all blow over. And then we'd move to Devon, where I'd definitely never see him again.

I geared myself up to seeing Luke at the meeting and being really cool but, when I arrived in the prefab, Sian was the only one there, bent over some notes at one of the tables.

"Hey," I said as I walked in. "Others not here yet?"

Sian shook her head. "Not coming," she said. "Luke wants to go over some things with Olivia. I guess we're not wanted."

I felt a mixture of relief and disappointment. "Oh, okay," I said, and put my rucksack down next to hers on the table.

Sian looked agitated. "Do you think he fancies Olivia?"

"*Olivia?* Er, I don't think so. They've been mates a long time. She told me. He's a friend of her brother."

Sian sighed, then shifted some papers around. After a few moments, she looked up at me. "T. J., can I talk to you?"

"Sure."

"Promise you won't tell anyone?"

Oh no, I thought. She's going to tell me about her crush on Luke. I shook my head. "No, I won't tell anyone."

"It's about Luke," she started. No surprise there, I thought as I sat at the desk and waited to hear all about her unrequited love. "He . . . well, we . . ."

"You like him, don't you?" I asked. I thought I'd make it easy for her. We were in the same situation after all. She was clearly mixed-up, wondering if Luke was coming on to every girl he spent time with. She was worried about Olivia. I was worried about her.

She nodded. "I don't expect you to really be able to understand . . . ," she continued.

Ha! I thought. Little do you know, but you couldn't have picked anybody more perfect to understand. Emotionally we were twins. Both experiencing unrequited love. I decided that I'd hear her out and give her the same advice that Hannah had given me. Luke was a babe. Loads of people had crushes on him, but she had to try and get over it. Stay cool. Move on.

"See, it's really difficult . . . ," Sian continued.

"Yes . . ."

"I know Nesta's a mate of yours, so you mustn't tell her that I know, but he's going to finish with her. It's not working out with them."

"Really?" I was surprised that he'd told her. Strange, I thought. But then maybe I was so unhelpful on Sunday that he felt he had to go somewhere else for advice or a shoulder to cry on.

Sian nodded. "Yes. I do feel bad about it, but then,

what's happening with us is so strong that, well, he couldn't carry on with Nesta, it wouldn't be fair to her."

D'oh, I thought. Am I missing something here? "Er . . . what do you mean what's happening with you?"

"Me and Luke."

Poor Sian, I thought. She really imagines that she has a chance but, after what he said to me about her, she's going to get badly let down.

"Sian," I said. "I know Luke is lovely, but I reckon he gets a lot of people fancying him. And he's so open and friendly with everyone, sometimes it's possible to get the wires crossed, if you know what I mean. Read too much into things. You have to take care of yourself. You don't want to get your hopes up, then get hurt when nothing happens."

"Oh, I'm sure I've not got my wires crossed. . . ."

God, she has it bad, I thought. She really has been reading a lot into the time she's spent with him.

"Sian, Luke's a very touchy-feely kind of guy. It doesn't always mean anything, and it has to be a two-way thing for it to work."

"I know. And it is."

"But how do you know that when nothing's happened between you?"

"But it *has* happened. He came over on Monday

night. Now I've no doubt that he feels the same."

I felt a horrible lurch in the pit of my stomach. "But how?"

Sian looked coy for a moment. "He kissed me."

That shut me up. He *kissed* her? But . . . but, I thought, he told me that she was a poor mixed-up kid. That he could *never* fancy her.

"Oh, sorry, T. J. You looked shocked. I know Nesta's your friend. Sorry. We didn't mean for anyone to get hurt. But he is going to finish with her. He's just waiting for the right moment to tell her. Then we can be together."

I felt like my brain was going to explode. Could this have been what he wanted to talk to me about on Sunday? I asked myself. Not just finishing with Nesta, but starting to go out with Sian . . . ? No, surely not. But then . . . maybe. Oh God. How could I have been such a *fool*? Talk about getting your wires crossed, misreading the signals. I get the prize. All ready to tell Sian what an idiot she was with her unreciprocated love and how it was all in her head, when all along it was me that had it in *my* head, and I couldn't have been more wrong about everything. Oh God. I'd been so sure that there was something special between us. All those longing looks he gave me. Then again . . . maybe he's playing everyone along. Me, Sian, Nesta. All of us. No. He's not like that. It's all in my stupid head. He'd kissed Sian, hadn't he? But then . . . it can't be that special between them if she's worried about him spending time with Olivia. She can't be that sure of him. Maybe he's just notching girls up, seeing how many he can score. Olivia did warn me in the beginning. He likes to prove to himself that he can have anyone. No. No. He's a nice guy. Oh God, I feel confused.

E-mail: **Inbox (1)**
From: <u>hannahnutter@fastmail.com</u>
To: <u>babewithbrains@psnet.co.uk</u>
Date: 8 December
Subject: Dishy dude

Hey, dingbat features,

   What's happening over there? Hope all is okay with the Lukieminukie. Let me know.

Yours,
Hannahlulu

E-mail: **Outbox (1)**
From: babewithbrains@psnet.co.uk
To: hannahnutter@fastmail.com
Date: 10 December
Subject: Re: Dishy dude

Hi, Hannah,

   This is the worst day of my whole whole life. I've never felt so totally down and confused. Turns out Luke isn't into Nesta. Or me. He's into this strange-looking girl called Sian. At least I think he is. She just told me, they've kissed already. I was all ready to tell her that she was misreading the signals and was on a lost cause when she confessed that they'd snogged. You can misread someone holding your hand, but a snog's a snog. No misreading that. I feel a fool. Miserable. Stupid. Can't trust my own feelings, don't know if I can trust the signals I'm getting from Luke. Who can I trust?

Yours truly,
Foolish in Finchley

E-mail: **Inbox (1)**
From: hannahnutter@fastmail.com
To: babewithbrains@psnet.co.uk
Date: 10 December
Subject: Re: Dishy dude

ME! Idioto. You can trust me. Nothing is over until the fat lady sings or something like that. Listen. I've snogged people I don't fancy. Wrong place. Too much sun. Temporary loss of sanity. All sorts of reasons.

I think you ought to go and have it out with dishy dude. See what's really going on in his head regards to you, this Sian girl, and Nesta. You've got nothing to lose by the sound of it and, knowing you as I do, you aren't one to let your imagination get the better of you.

Keep me updated. Sounds like life over there is much more exciting than over here. Nothing's happening. Don't fancy anyone.

Très boooring. I feel like a nun. Nun of this, nun of that, geddit?

Love,
Sister Mary Conceptua Hannah

Chapter 13

Life Before
Boys

Horrible. Life can't get more horrible, I thought after I'd got home. The hour spent with Sian had been excruciating with her going on and on about Luke, not realizing that her every word was like rubbing salt into a wound.

"Supper's on the table," called Mum from the kitchen.

"Not hungry," I called back. "I'll have something later."

Much later, I thought. I felt sick, like I never wanted to eat again. I threw myself on my bed. I hate this feeling, I thought. I so want to be back to normal. Before Steve. Before Luke. Back when I was about eight and all I thought about boys was that they were noisy creatures who picked their noses, had smelly socks, and were to be avoided at all costs. It's rotten fancying boys. It's rotten being a teenager. It's rotten being me.

I replied to an e-mail from Hannah bringing her up-to-date on my latest nightmare, then I tried to do some homework, but my mind wouldn't concentrate. I attempted Izzie's meditation to calm myself, but peace of mind seemed a million miles away, and I couldn't get the image of Luke kissing Sian out of my head. I needed something to relax that was easy to do. An aromatic bath, I thought, that's supposed to be effective. Last time I'd seen her, Izzie had given me a list of oils from her essential oil book that you could add to the water to combat stress. I went and looked at my lotions and potions and found the one with lavender in it that Nesta had given me for my birthday. Lavender's one of the oils on the list, so I went and ran a bath, then poured in a few drops. It smelled delicious, but when I got in, I felt guilty lying there inhaling a lovely scent given to me by a friend who I knew I'd let down.

After my bath I checked my e-mails and luckily Hannah had replied quickly. Talk to Luke, she said. At first I thought, no way, I can't, and e-mailed her back saying so. What's the point? I had my chance to talk to him on Sunday and I blew it. I had the conversation with him in my head instead, imagining what he'd say. Over and over again. Each time, I changed the script. Maybe I should talk to Nesta? Tell her about Sian. She deserves to know. No. I can't do that. That's Luke's responsibility and besides, I don't really know what the story is or what's going on with them at all.

This is mad, I thought after a while. Why don't I just have it out with Luke? Hannah's right. I've got nothing to lose, not anymore. My sanity went weeks ago. Talk to him. Find out for once and for all what's going on, with Sian, with Nesta, with me.

I went to the phone, picked it up, then lost my nerve and put it down again.

After a few deep breaths, I picked it up again and dialled. My heart was thumping in my chest as it began to ring at his end.

"Hello," said an Indian-sounding voice.

"Um, is Luke there?"

"I'm afraid you have the wrong number, my dear," said the voice and the phone clicked off.

I checked the numbers, picked up the phone and dialed once more. I can do this, I can do this, I told myself as the phone began to ring at the other end. Just as I heard someone pick up, my bedroom door opened and Mum came in with some cheese on toast on a plate. I almost had a heart attack and quickly slammed down the phone.

"Mum!"

"Sorry, love, were you talking to someone?"

"*No.* I mean yes, I mean . . . finished."

Mum put the plate on my desk, then sat on the end of my bed. "Is everything all right, T. J.?"

"Yeah. Course. Why?"

"Just you haven't seemed your usual self lately. Is something bothering you?"

"No. Fine, everything's fine. Been busy. School project. And course, thinking about Devon. But, yes, everything's fine."

Mum sighed and got up. "Eat up your supper, and I'll bring you a cup of tea," she said as she went to the door where she paused. "If you need to talk to me about anything, I'm always here."

For a brief moment, I thought I would talk to her. She'd been a teenager once, many lifetimes ago. Maybe she went through something like this. Maybe she'd understand. I was just about to open my mouth when the phone rang, causing me to jump again.

"Are you going to get that?" asked Mum.

I nodded and picked up the extension. It was Luke.

I put my hand over the receiver. "For me," I whispered to Mum.

Mum nodded and left me to it.

"Hey, Watts," said Luke. "Did you just ring me?"

"Er, no, that is, yeah. . . ."

"Thought so. The phone went, but when I picked

up there was no one there, so I rang star sixty-nine and it gave me your number.'

"Oh yeah, just my m . . . I got disturbed."

"So what can I do for you?"

I took a deep breath and decided to go for it. "I just left Sian," I said, then waited for him to tell me what had happened with them.

"So?" he said after a pause.

"So, she told me what happened between you."

Luke laughed or rather snorted at the other end. "I bet she did."

"So you're not denying it."

"Hey, Watts," said Luke. "I *told* you that she had a crush on me."

"Yeah, but she says you feel the same way."

"Yeah, right," Luke snorted again.

"She said you kissed her."

"Oh *did* she now?"

"Well, did you or didn't you?"

"Would you care either way, Watts?"

"Me? No, course not. Just after what you were saying the other day, about Nesta . . ."

"Listen," said Luke in a serious tone, "Sian kissed *me*. There's a difference. No way was it a two-way thing, if you get what I mean. She took me unaware, invited me round saying she wanted to go through the Highgate side of things on the project and me, like a total fool, fell for it. I told you, no way would

I fancy Sian. She's just not my type. No way. It's all in her head."

"She thinks you're going to go out with her after you've finished with Nesta."

I could hear Luke sigh. "Bugger," he said. "I'm going to have to tell her straight, aren't I?"

"Dunno," I said. "I guess." My mind was reeling. I *wanted* to believe him. It did sound like he was telling the truth, but there was a niggling feeling at the back of my mind telling me that something wasn't right.

"I really didn't kiss her," said Luke as if picking up on my need for more reassurance. "I let her kiss me for, like . . . a nanosecond. I didn't want to . . . you know, like . . . push her off. That would have been cruel. It can be hard knowing how to play it sometimes. How do you let someone down? I mean, she's a sweet kid, and I didn't want to hurt her. You must know how it can be. Sometimes you do the kissing, sometimes you are kissed, sometimes it's totally mutual. But no way was it with Sian."

I felt weird talking about different types of kisses with Luke. It brought too many images up in my mind. Which I *did* like. So there was nothing to the kiss with Sian. Once again, Hannah had been right, and it was possible to get into a situation where you ended up snogging (or being snogged by) someone you didn't want to be with. So he didn't fancy her, but I still didn't know what he felt about *me*. I should ask him, I thought, but I didn't know how to begin. I needed time to think about how to phrase it without dropping myself in it and looking a total prat. But I needed to know. I needed to know really badly if what I'd been feeling over the last few weeks had all been in my imagination, or whether he felt the same way.

"Listen, Luke . . ."

"Yeah?"

"Um . . . tomorrow, after school . . . er . . . could you, could we meet up?"

"You asking me on a date, Watts?"

"*No.* Course not. No date. Talk." Then I wondered when my use of English had disintegrated to Tarzan speak—like me Tarzan, you Jane. Me T. J. You Luke. Ugabuga. I am beyond help, I thought.

Luke laughed. "Oh. No date? Talk," he said. "Why can't we talk now?"

"Um . . . not on the phone. I . . . I want to see you in person."

"Hmm. Sounds serious, Watts. Okay. Yeah, I can do that. Be good. What time?" His voice sounded warm.

"About seven? Under the trees in Pond Square."

"I'll be there," he said.

Essential Oils to Aid Relaxation

Add six to eight drops to the bath water as it is running. Swish the oil around so that it doesn't all stay in one spot.

> Camomile
> Cedarwood
> Clary sage
> Lavender
> Marjoram
> Neroli
> Patchouli
> Petitgrain
> Rose
> Rosewood
> Sandalwood
> Ylang-ylang

Chapter 14

Earth to
Planet Watts

The following day at school, I felt like I was floating on a cloud. A dark cloud full of thunder, rain, and lightning maybe, but a cloud none the less, and my state of mind didn't go unnoticed.

"Are you with us, Theresa Joanne?" asked Miss Watkins in PSHE.

"And what's so exciting out there, Miss Watts?" asked Mr. Johnson in English, when he caught me gazing out of the window.

"Calling T. J. Watts, T. J. *Watts*," said Mrs. Elwes in art. "Earth to planet Watts. Come back."

I had so much to consider. Moving to Devon was still on the agenda, and my life and all its complications here might soon all be behind me. I wasn't sure how I felt about that. It kept changing. And Steve. I'd hardly seen him since the project began, and although we usually only met on the weekends, we did generally talk on the phone during the week. We'd both been busy, and he had a lot on with his photography team, but I wondered if he'd minded that I hadn't been calling as often as usual. And then there was Luke. Part of me felt anxious about the meeting with him tonight and part of me felt a rush of excitement. In case any of the girls sussed my strange state of mind and started asking questions, I made my excuses at lunchtime and buried myself in research in the library. They were cool about it. Everyone involved in the project was under pressure as the presentation of our work so far was next week, so we had to get everything finished.

After school I dashed home to get ready. I felt so nervous. I'd never felt like this when I was going to meet Steve. It was like I'd drunk about six cups of strong coffee and I was buzzing.

I decided to wear my combats, a T-shirt, and my parka jacket as it would be cold outside. Then I combed my hair loose instead of wearing it like I usually did—scraped back in a plait. A quick slick of lip gloss, a squirt of perfume, and I was ready.

About ten minutes before leaving, I heard the doorbell go then, a few moments later, Mum called up the stairs.

"T. J. Steve's here for you. And Dad and I are off to our concert now. See you later."

Steve! Omigod! I thought as I heard his footsteps coming up the stairs. What am I going to say? A moment later, my bedroom door opened and in he walked.

"Hey, you look nice," he said as he stooped to give me a kiss, but I had leaned in to give him a hug and turned slightly so that his kiss landed on my cheek. I turned my face back so that he could kiss me on the lips but by then he'd backed off.

"Oh. Thanks."

"Going out?"

I nodded.

"Where?"

"Um, Highgate. Um, project stuff."

"Want me to come?" asked Steve. "Keep you company?"

I felt like a fly caught in a web. "Um. Nah. It will be boring. You know, meeting schmeeting."

Steve looked disappointed. "Meeting Luke?"

I nodded again. Steve shrugged then reached into the bag he was carrying and pulled out a postcard and a photo. "Thought you might like to see these."

I bent over to look as Steve laid them out on my desk.

"The painting is called *Work,* and it's by Ford Madox Brown," he explained as I looked at the postcard of an old-fashioned painting showing some men with rolled-up sleeves digging. "It's really famous." Then he pointed to the photograph. "And *here* is the place he painted."

"Oh, wow," I said as I compared the two. "It's on Greenhill, just off Hampstead High Street. It's where Mum always parks when we go shopping there."

"I know. It's amazing, isn't it? I thought it would look good as part of your display."

"It will. Thank you *so* much," I said glancing at my watch.

"Sorry. Am I keeping you? It's just I was passing, and I . . . well, when I made the connection, I couldn't wait to show you." He reached into his rucksack again and got out more photos. "Plus here's all the shots of houses where famous people lived."

I took a quick glance at them, and they looked fabulous. He'd clearly spent a lot of time going round photographing for me. I felt rotten. "Steve, these are brilliant. Look, I'm so sorry I'm in such a hurry, but I've got to go. I'm supposed to be in Highgate at seven."

Steve went to the door. "No problem. I'll walk down with you."

I felt like the Queen of Mean. I could see that he was making a great effort to be cheerful, like he was cool about everything, but the atmosphere felt strained and unnatural. Mean, mean, mean, a voice in my head said. For a moment, I thought about calling Luke and canceling. I didn't want to see Steve hurt, not for a moment, but Luke would have already left, and I knew that if I put our meeting off, it would only prolong the agony I was going through in my head.

When we got to the end of the road, I gave Steve an extra big hug. "Speak to you later?" I asked. "Maybe we can do something tomorrow."

"Yeah, sure," said Steve lightly. "Yeah. See you around, T. J."

And he walked off in the opposite direction. I could see by the way he hunched his shoulders up that I'd upset him. Maybe Izzie has the right idea, I thought as he disappeared around a corner. Celibacy. Or maybe I should take a tip from Hannah. Become a nun. It would be a hell of a lot easier to opt out of the dating game altogether. It was painful no matter what side you were on.

I got to Pond Square at about ten past seven, but there was no sign of Luke. I checked my watch again and looked round. I waited until half past and still no sign. I didn't want to ring in case I sounded desperate, but by seven forty-five I was freezing and my toes had turned to blocks of ice. I've been stood up, I thought. And it serves me right. I decided to give him another few minutes, then I called his number.

His mum answered.

"Er, is Luke there?" I asked.

"Yes," she said. "But he's asleep. Nodded off in front of the telly. Shall I wake him?"

Asleep? I thought. *Asleep*!! "Er, no, don't wake him. I'll catch him later."

"It's Sian, isn't it?" said Mrs. De Biasi. "I'll tell him you called."

"No, not Sian. Er, no. Don't worry. It's not important. I'll catch him later."

I clicked my phone off and sank on to one of the benches. I didn't want to talk to anyone while I was feeling this low. Izzie would probably say this was karma. She says that the law of karma is that what you sow, so shall you reap. In plain English, you get what you deserve. And I probably deserved this. I'd blown Steve out, and now Luke had blown me out. But *asleep*! I couldn't believe it. And his mum knew Sian's name. She obviously called there a lot. Well, there's your answer T. J. Watts, I thought. That's exactly how much this meeting mattered to Luke. So much that he fell asleep and forgot. I got up and wearily trudged down the road to the bus stop. God, I hate feeling this way, I thought. Maybe I will be a nun or join those Hare Krishna people who renounce the world, shave their heads, and hand people carnations at airports. Anything, *anything* has to be easier than this.

Work was painted by the Pre-Raphaelite painter Ford Madox Brown between 1852–1865 and depicts navvies digging sewers in Hampstead. It is currently hanging in the Manchester City Art Gallery in Manchester, England.

Chapter 15

Tempting
Trouble

When I got home, the house was quiet, as Mum and Dad were still at their concert at the Barbican. Mojo was curled up on the sofa in the sitting room, and he looked up with a guilty expression when he heard me come in. He knew he wasn't supposed to sleep on the furniture as he had his own basket in the kitchen, but as soon as Mum and Dad went out, he always made himself comfortable on the sofa.

"Don't get up, Mojo," I said as I sat next to him. He took a long look at me, then got up and licked my face. He let out a soft whine as if to say he understood, then curled up, leaning against my legs with his paw up over my knees. He's amazing when I'm feeling low. It's like he picks up on it, then likes to stay as close as possible to me as if trying to comfort me.

"Rough," I said to him.

"Rff," he agreed and sank his head onto my lap.

I switched on the TV and flicked channels for a while, but none of the programs registered. My concentration was all over the place. After a while, I curled up with Mojo and closed my eyes and I must have nodded off, because the next thing I knew, I was awoken by the doorbell ringing. I checked my watch. Nine o'clock. Too early for Mum and Dad to be back, plus they never went out without their keys. I went to the window and peeked out from behind the curtain. My heart skipped a beat when I saw Luke standing there. Seeing a movement at the window, he glanced over as I darted back out of sight. The doorbell rang again. A long insistent ring. Then I heard his voice through the letterbox.

"T. J. *T. J.* I know you're in there."

I tiptoed into the hall. The letterbox flicked open, and I could see his eyes looking through.

"Go away," I said.

"T. J. Let me in."

"I don't want to talk to you."

"Please, T. J. Look, you've every right to be mad. I'm sorry I stood you up. I didn't mean to. I don't know what happened. I crashed out on the sofa, and the next thing I know, it was past eight. I tried ringing your mobile. When you didn't answer, I came straight over. I'm *really* sorry. Let me in."

By this time, Mojo had come to see what all the noise was about. He looked at me, then at the letter-box, then back at me as if to say, what kind of creature is so small they can look through a letterbox?

"Chow, Mojo," called Luke, causing Mojo to go over to the door and try to lick him through the letterbox. Then I heard him say, "Ey*uck*."

I had to laugh. Mojo's tail was wagging like mad, then he positioned himself on the mat inside so that he was eyeball-to-eyeball with Luke.

"Come on, T. J., please," said Luke. "I'm down on my knees here." Then he laughed. "I really am, too. And making eyeball contact with your dog, much as I like him, is *not* why I came over."

"Five minutes," I said firmly as I went to let him in. I felt genuinely mad with him. I'd had enough. More than enough, and now I just wanted my life and my sanity back. As always Luke was supertuned in to how I was feeling.

"Mad with me, huh?" he said as he stood up with a big cheesy grin.

I wasn't going to give in easily. "You could say that. I waited for ages. I was freezing."

"I really am sorry. I meant to be there. Usually I'm Mr. Reliable. I don't normally fall asleep early evening, but lately . . . dunno, I haven't been sleeping well . . . lot on my mind . . ."

"Tell me about it," I said as I went back into the sitting room.

Luke followed me in. "T. J. . . ."

"Your mum thought I was Sian. She knows there's someone called Sian all right, doesn't she?"

"Yeah, but I told you that's a one-way thing," said Luke following me in. "Totally in her head."

I didn't ask him to sit down as I didn't want him staying, so we stood at opposing ends of the room, like boxers sizing each other up in the ring. "I'm not so sure anymore. I mean, how do I know if I can trust you? You play with people's feelings, and I don't think you know how it affects them."

"Hey, that's not fair. I never encouraged Sian."

"You let her massage you, I'd say that's pretty encouraging."

"Not in my house. Everyone's always giving everyone neck and back rubs. It means nothing."

Oh, I thought, so did that mean that my giving him a neck rub meant nothing as well?

"So what about Nesta then? You've certainly encouraged her, and she has no idea that you plan to finish with her. If that's not playing with people's feelings, I don't know what is."

"Yeah, but . . ."

"And you're a flirt, Luke De Biasi. I've seen you, holding girls' hands, playing the confidante to Sian. I think you probably like the attention."

"Look, T. J., I've told you before. There's nothing going on with Sian. *Nothing.*"

"Yeah, like you said it wasn't working out with Nesta, but I don't see you getting round to letting her in on it."

Luke sighed. "Ah, well, that's difficult," he said. "I hate letting people down. And, anyway, you're still seeing Steve, so you're one to talk."

"Steve! *Steve?* What's he got to do with it? Why wouldn't I be seeing Steve?"

Luke looked directly into my eyes. "Because of us!"

"Us! *Us?* What's that supposed to mean? What us?"

"You know that what's happening with *us* is on another level."

That did it. I don't often lose my temper, but this time I saw red. "Stop saying that! And what does it mean exactly? On another level? What level? It could mean *anything.* What am I supposed to *think?* You use expressions like that, and it can be interpreted any *way,* it's no wonder Sian thinks you're into her. You probably told her that what you have with her is on another level as well."

Luke sank down on to the sofa. "Just going down to another level." He grinned up at me.

I didn't laugh at his joke.

"I've never given Sian anything to go on," he said. "Honestly."

"Okay. Honestly then. What about Nesta? How do you feel about her? Really?"

"It's over. I know, I know I haven't told her yet, but how can I? You of all people know how difficult it's going to be."

"There you go again. Why would *I* of all people know?"

Luke reached out, caught my hand, and pulled me toward him. "Come on, T. J., you can't deny it."

"Deny *what*?" I asked as I pulled away from him.

"Please, T. J., sit down," said Luke, patting the cushion on the sofa next to him. I didn't want to look at him as, although I was still mad, I couldn't deny the chemistry in the room. The air was so thick, you could have cut it with a knife. Instead of sitting next to him, I sat on the floor to the right of his feet, with my back to him, and folded my arms.

He moved over so that he was positioned behind me, with me sitting between his knees, then he put his hands on my shoulders.

"Come on, Watts," he said. "You know that there's something pretty special going on between us. I know you do."

He started to gently massage my shoulders and the back of my neck. I felt myself freeze, but when he began to play with my hair, it sent warm shivers up my spine. It felt amazing and was starting to feel dangerous. I tried to shrug him off.

"Come on, relax," he said softly. "Let me give you a neck rub. You need to chill out a bit. Relax."

What he'd just said to me about us having something special had caused my brain to fuse. I didn't know what else to say so I just sat there, letting him gently stroke my neck and my hair. It felt like my mind had gone totally blank, and everything had been turned off or tuned out except the sensation of him close behind me and the warmth of his hands on my shoulders.

After a moment he got up and went over to the CD player.

"Got any good CDs?"

"Erghh. Not sure," I said. "Mine are all upstairs, but I think there are a few of my brother's somewhere about. He left them here when he took off on his travels. They're there on the right of the player." Yes, I thought. Music. Good idea. Anything to distract me from the feelings that are running riot through me.

He picked out a CD, put it in the player, and switched it on.

"I think you'll like this one," he said as he sat behind me once again and resumed his gentle kneading on my shoulders.

As the CD began to play, I could hardly believe what I was hearing. I'd never heard the band before, but it was the perfect choice. Strings filled the room, then some piano, then the lyrics. All about dancing into the fire, eager to catch the flame. Tempting trouble, ready to play the game.

As the music filled the room, Luke's hands on my shoulders suddenly stopped massaging, and he turned me round to face him and put one hand under my chin, so that I had to look up at him. As our eyes met, I felt myself start to lose resistance, like I'd turned to rubber. He leaned toward me, slipped his hands under my arms, and pulled me up next to him. Then he leaned in again, and it was like everything went into slow motion, his face gradually coming closer to mine. I felt like I was melting into him, then his lips touched mine. I so wanted to respond, but suddenly I saw Nesta's face in my mind's eye, and Steve.

"No . . . *no,* Luke, we mustn't. There's Nesta and Steve to think about. Even if we do break up with them, this can only cause bad feelings."

Luke let out a soft moan. "T. J., you're *killing* me. *This* is killing me."

He looked so sad sitting there. I hated to see him like that and realized that I hadn't thought about his feelings. He looked at me pleadingly and took my hand again. "T. J., please. I can't go on like this."

"But . . . Nesta . . ."

"I'll tell Nesta. I promise. I will. Come here. . . ."

This time, as he pulled me toward him and put his

arms round my waist, I reached up, put my arms around his neck and his face moved toward mine again and, at last, we were kissing properly. A long, deep, soft kiss. Nothing else existed. It was like everything went black, and all I felt was the most sublime sensation of his lips on mine and his body close. Ecstasy.

After a few moments, he pulled away and smiled. "I've wanted to do that for a very long time. You okay with this?"

I was more than okay. I felt like I was in heaven. All I wanted was more, and I leaned forward and kissed him again.

We must have spent at least the next two hours with our arms around each other, cuddling and kissing until my jaw was sore. I'd never felt anything like it before—kissing Steve had never been like this. I wanted it to go on forever and ever.

We were cuddled up with my head on his chest, holding hands, listening to another CD, when we heard my parents' car pull up into the front drive. I leaped up in a panic. I'd completely lost track of time. I glanced at my watch. It was almost twelve. We'd been there for three hours.

"Oh God, they'll *kill* me."

"Back door?" said Luke, springing up and heading for the hall.

"Kitchen," I said as we both legged it to the back of the house.

As I let him out into the garden, he gave me a quick kiss, and both of us got the giggles. Then, as we heard the key in the front door, he sprinted across the garden. "See you, Watts."

"T. J., T. J.? Are you there?" asked Mum coming straight through into the kitchen. "What are you doing up?"

"Um. Just giving Mojo some fresh air in the garden," I replied as I came in and began locking the back door.

Mojo chose this moment to come through from the sitting room so blowing my story. Mum looked at me, then at the dog.

"But . . ."

"Oh *there* you are," I said, then giggled. I felt drunk. "Bad Mojo. Come on, boy." I began to unbolt the door.

Mojo wagged his tail and made for the garden.

"For heaven's sake, close that door," said Dad coming through to join us. "It's letting all the cold air in." Then he looked at me. "What's the matter with your face?"

"Face?" I said, putting my hand up to my chin. It did feel a bit raw. Oh God, I thought, I've got a snog rash. "What do you mean?"

"Your face," said Dad taking a closer look. "It's all red round your jawline."

"Oh, that!" I said, grinning like an idiot. "Oh

yeah. Er, I did a facial before. Got a bit carried away with the exfoliator and, er, clearing any blackheads."

Dad pulled a face and Mum was looking at me quizzically as I made for the hall and stairs. I don't think she believed a word of it. Better get out of here quick, I thought, before they suss out what I've really been doing. Lying on the sofa snogging a boy who wasn't even my boyfriend all evening probably wouldn't go down too well in their book.

Later, when I lay in my bed in a mild stupor, still smiling all over my face, I thought, This can't be wrong. This is the real thing. It really is. And I, T. J. Watts, for the first time in my life, am totally and utterly in love.

E-mail: **Outbox (1)**
From: babewithbrains@psnet.co.uk
To: hannahnutter@fastmail.com
Date: 12 December
Subject: True Love

Dear Hannah,

It's one o'clock in the morning here, and I can't sleep. I had to tell you as I have to tell someone. I am in love. Really, really in love. It's official. Luke came over this evening, and I had the best night of my entire life. I think he is my soulmate. And what is even better, he feels the same way. He wasn't into Sian after all. It is awesome. I can't sleep thinking about him. I am also going to e-mail Steve as I think it's only fair to him that I tell him as soon as possible, and I don't want him to hear from anyone else. Plus he is a nice guy. I will follow it up in person as I know it's mean to dump someone by e-mail, but I can't run the risk of someone else telling him first, and I'd hate for that to happen.

Lots of love,
T. J.

E-mail: **Outbox (1)**
From: babewithbrains@psnet.co.uk
To: jamesblonde@psnet.co.uk
Date: 12 December
Subject: Us

Dear Steve,

I'm writing to tell you that I can't go out with you anymore. I'm really sorry, and I hope you won't be too upset. It's not you, I think you're fantastic. It's me. But I'm not going to insult you by explaining or trying to make excuses. It's never easy ending something, and I'm keeping this short as it's about the hundredth version I've written, and I couldn't find the right words in any of them.

I hope you will always be my friend as you genuinely do mean a lot to me, and I really enjoyed going out with you, and I'm sorry to do this by e-mail, but will explain why I had to do it this way later.

Your friend,
T. J.

Chapter 16

Snog
Rash

"God, what happened?" asked Izzie the next day at
school as she stared at the rash on my face. "Did
something bite you?"

"Sort of, er, but not bite," I replied sheepishly. I'd
tried everything I could find in the bathroom when
I'd got up. Mum's soothing creams, Germaline. Aloe
vera gel. But my face was still inflamed, and the creams
only irritated it more.

Izzie looked puzzled.

"Snog rash," I said.

"Oh! Steve not been shaving? I hate it when boys
have that scratchy stubble. It can really hurt. I'll see if
there's a balm or something in my essential oil book
for you."

I shook my head. "It wasn't Steve."

"So who . . . ? Omigod. Was it who I think it . . . ?"

I nodded. "We couldn't help it, Izzie. We tried not to, but . . . it was too strong. He's going to tell Nesta. And I've already told Steve. Do you think I should tell Nesta?"

Izzie shook her head vehemently. "No way. That's Luke's responsibility. Are you *sure* about this?"

"Hundred percent. I've never felt like this before. It is totally *totally* amazing. Everything was . . . just perfect. I think Luke's my soulmate."

Izzie let out a sigh. "Wow! Carumba! I thought you were the one who didn't believe in soulmates."

"I know, but that was before Luke. It's like everything you and Lucy said . . . and more."

"Double wow. What can I say?"

"Do you hate me?"

"No. Course not. If he's your soulmate, you can't argue with destiny, but hell, poor you and poor Nesta. It's not going to be easy. I'd lie low if I were you in case Luke's told Nesta already. Stay out of her way until she's calmed down."

Not going to be easy. That's an understatement, I thought as Izzie went off to the cloakrooms to hang up her coat.

Lucy wasn't as friendly when she arrived in the school hall five minutes later and confronted me straight away. "Steve told me that you dumped him. On e-mail, too. That's a bit cold, isn't it? I'd have thought you could have at least told him to his face."

I looked at the floor. She was right. I knew it had been a lousy way to dump someone, but then I wasn't thinking straight last night, and it seemed the right thing to do at the time. In the light of the day, I wished I'd waited—like who was I thinking was going to tell Steve about Luke and me in the middle of the night? I guess love can make you go a bit doolally, I thought. I'd felt so high and so good last night that I thought everything would just work out, everyone would understand. It's true love and to be forgiven anything. When I woke up this morning, I cursed myself for having been so impetuous. If we lived in the old days of letters, I could have ripped it up, but with e-mail, one press of the button, and it's gone forever.

"I'm sorry, Lucy. I know it wasn't one of my best ideas, but I . . . I wanted him to know as soon as possible, in case he heard from . . . from anyone else."

"Why? Why as soon as possible? Have you met someone else?"

I nodded. "I am sorry, Lucy. I didn't want to hurt him more than necessary. Is he okay? How is he?"

"How do you think? He really liked you."

"I know. I really liked him, too. I still do. And that's

why I thought it best he was told as soon as possible. It wasn't fair not to. The . . . er, the chemistry wasn't there anymore, and I didn't want to lie to him. Surely you agree with that?"

Lucy didn't look convinced. "Whatever, but there are ways of letting someone down. So, who's the new boy? You've been keeping him pretty quiet."

"Oh . . . just someone . . ."

"Must be pretty special for you to end it with Steve by e-mail."

"He is. *Very* special, just . . . he was . . . is involved with someone as well, and we don't want to go public until he's finished with his girlfriend as well."

Lucy looked miffed. "Fine. Whatever. Don't tell me, then."

"Lucy, I *can't* tell you yet. . . ."

"I *hate* secrets, and I thought that we were mates. . . ."

Just at that moment Nesta bounded up behind us. I felt myself cower inwardly. I didn't know if Luke had told her, and if he had, whether he'd have mentioned me or not.

"Hey." She smiled, then noticed my face. "Hey, hey, T. J. Watts. Do I see what I think I see? Uno snog rash. Hmm. Looks like someone had fun. I didn't think Steve had it in him."

"Snog rash?" said Lucy studying my face carefully.

"Oh, yeah. Wow. You don't waste time do you?"

"What are you on about?" said Nesta. "She's been going with Steve for ages."

"Not Steve," said Lucy. "T. J.'s finished with Steve and got herself a new boyfriend. And she won't tell me who."

Nesta raised an eyebrow. "Oh really? Won't tell, huh?" she said, then leaned over and pulled my arm behind my back, like she was a policeman and she was arresting me. "Ve have vays of making you talk, Miss Vatts. Come on, Lucy, we'll get it out of her someway or another."

I laughed and tried to play along with her like everything was normal. Clearly Luke hadn't told her yet, but then it was only the morning after, and he had probably decided that the right way to do it was face-to-face instead of e-mail. As we were scuffling about in the corridor, Izzie came out of the cloakrooms and flew toward us.

"Hey, leave her alone," she said, pulling us apart. "She didn't mean to hurt anyone."

Nesta let go of me and we all stared at Izzie for a moment. She quickly realized her mistake. From her angle, when she came out of the cloakrooms, it must have looked as if Lucy and Nesta were pushing me about.

"Izzie, they were only messing about . . . ," I explained.

"Yeah. She has a new lover boy and won't say who," said Lucy.

"And why on earth would we push T. J. about?" asked Nesta. "Are you on *drugs*?"

I shook my head at Izzie to try to tell her not to say. Unluckily, Lucy saw me.

"You know who, don't you Izzie?" asked Lucy.

Nesta pouted. "So how come you told Izzie but not us?" she asked. "I thought we were all mates. Why can't we know as well?"

Izzie looked lost for words as Lucy and Nesta looked at her accusingly. Then Lucy looked at me, and her eyes narrowed. I could see the penny drop for her.

"Oh, no," she gasped. "Oh, no. T. J.?"

"What? *What*?" demanded Nesta. "What *is* going on with you guys this morning?"

Lucy's expression grew cold. "Nothing. Come on, Nesta, let's go."

She linked her arm through Nesta's and pulled her away toward the assembly hall.

Izzie looked at me and grimaced. "Hells bells and poo," she said. "The shitola has just hit the fan."

I wanted to turn around and run. The warm glow that had been surrounding me since last night suddenly evaporated and was replaced by a cold feeling of doom. Why, oh why, does love have to be so complicated? I asked myself as Izzie pushed me gently in the direction of assembly.

Lucy hauled Nesta off as soon as assembly had finished, and I saw them heading for the cloakrooms just as the bell for lessons went. I wanted to run out of the school gates and go home and hide, but how would I explain that to anyone? I can't exactly see my mum giving me a note to excuse me from lessons.

"Just tell her the truth," said Izzie. "She can only kill you."

I nodded. "I will. Should I catch up with them?"

Izzie nodded back. "Best get it over with. Want me to come with you?"

"Please."

As we made our way to the cloakrooms, I remembered a scene from a film I'd seen with a condemned man walking to the electric chair. *Dead Man Walking,* it was called. "Dead girl walking," I said to Izzie as she put her arm through mine.

"Just keep breathing," said Izzie, who looked as worried as I felt.

Nesta and Lucy had their heads close together in the corner of the cloakrooms, and they looked up as I walked in. Luckily we were the only ones in there, which was a relief as I'd have hated anyone else from our class to have been there, earwigging it all then passing it round the school.

Lucy looked at me defiantly. "I had to tell her, T. J.

It's only fair. You said Steve deserved to know as soon as possible, so Nesta does too and"—at this point she gave Izzie a dirty look—"and no one else round here was brave enough."

I glanced at Izzie, who looked shocked, then at Nesta. "I really am sorry. . . ."

Nesta shrugged. "Yeah. So am I. But no worries, T. J., I know it must be difficult for you, and I'm sorry it's had to come out this way. . . ."

I didn't understand and looked at the girls quizzically.

"She already knew," explained Lucy.

"You *already* knew?" I asked. So Luke had told her? "When? When did he tell you?"

"Oh, ages ago, when you guys first started working on the project together. . . ."

Whadtt? I thought. He never mentioned it to me. Last night he'd said he hadn't told her yet.

Nesta put her hand on my arm and looked at me sympathetically. "It must be really tough for you. . . ."

Tough for *me*? I thought. What the hell was going on? "What exactly did Luke tell you?"

"Oh, you know." Nesta sighed. "About you having a crush on him. He told me all about it, as he didn't know how to deal with it. He said he didn't want to hurt your feelings as you were a mate of mine. . . . And I didn't want to say anything to you as I didn't want to hurt your feelings either. I mean, it *is* kind of embarrassing, isn't it? I know you're into Steve, so fancying Luke? No way. I knew that you'd never make a play for him. In fact, I even wondered if he'd got the wrong end of the stick. You know, inflated male ego and all that."

"I . . . I . . . so why did he say anything?"

"He said he wanted to let me know in *case* you got the wrong idea about him. He says it happens all the time, that girls misread the signals. He wanted to reassure me that your crush was all in your head. He told me that what he and I have is on another level and not to worry."

I felt like someone had plunged a knife into me. "But . . . but . . . I . . . oh, God. What a mess. I . . . So, you haven't spoken to him today then?"

"Today? No."

"Oh, God, I'm so sorry, Nesta. . . ."

"No need to apologize. I'm glad it's all out in the open now, and we can talk about it. And I totally understand. Luke is gorgeous, and as I said, loads of girls have crushes on him. I can't say I blame you. . . ."

Lucy didn't look as forgiving and looked accusingly at my chin. "But that doesn't explain . . ." She didn't finish her sentence and looked away, but not before Nesta had noticed where she'd been looking.

I saw confusion flicker in Nesta's eyes. Izzie looked horrified, not as horrified as I felt, though. I felt mad with Luke. He'd given us both the same line. We were both on another level then? No. No. I knew it wasn't like that. Not after last night. It was special, a once-in-a-lifetime thing.

Nesta sighed heavily. "I'd forgotten . . . Steve didn't give you that snog rash, did he?"

I didn't answer.

"I suppose he likes you because you're so clever," said Nesta sadly. "Beauty and brains, I always said it was a lethal combination."

"But . . . ," I started. Just at that moment, the door opened, and Miss Watkins stuck her head round the door.

"Theresa Watts, Izzie Foster, Lucy Lovering, Nesta Williams. What are you doing in here? Didn't you hear the bell? Move yourselves. Now!"

As we filed out after her, my heart was thumping in my chest. I felt angry.

I need to talk to Luke, I thought, as soon as possible. Find out what he's been saying, and give him a piece of my mind.

I sat through Miss Watkins's class in agony. Lucy and Nesta were sitting behind and I looked round whenever I could to try and gauge what was going on in their heads. Lucy stared steadfastly in front of her and wouldn't let me catch her eye. Nesta looked upset and was doodling on her notebook. Izzie also kept looking round, then glancing over at me and rolling her eyes.

"Izzie Foster," said Miss Watkins. "What is so interesting at the back of the class today? Maybe you'd like to share it with the rest of us."

"Er, no, nothing, Miss," stuttered Izzie. "Sorry."

"If you don't start paying proper attention, you'll stay behind and do detention. Understood?"

"Understood," said Izzie, and put her nose in her book.

I felt utterly miserable. Lucy and Nesta would probably never speak to me again, and I'd managed to get Izzie in trouble, not only with Miss Watkins but also with Lucy. She'd made it very clear in the cloakrooms that she thought that Izzie should have said something to Nesta about Luke and me. My new best friends, I thought, and I was going to lose them. That is, if I hadn't lost them already.

At break Nesta obviously had the same idea as I did. I watched as she dived out of the classroom, with Lucy in hot pursuit, then get her mobile out of her bag.

I waited until the classroom had emptied except for Izzie, who had hung back to stay with me. I quickly pulled out my mobile and dialed Luke's number. I had to warn him. Plus I had to find out what was really going on. I got his voicemail.

"Hell, voicemail," I said. "I think Nesta's gotten through first."

"Try again," urged Izzie. "He might not be on

break yet, so might have it switched off. Sometimes breaktime is different in different schools."

I sat there dialing. And dialing. And dialing again. Suddenly I heard the phone ring, and Luke's voice at the other end.

"Luke," I said.

"Hey, Watts," he said cheerfully. "Top night last night."

"Yeah, right. I thought so too at the time."

"Hey. What's the problem? Your voice sounds weird. What do you mean?"

"Have you said anything to Nesta yet about you breaking up with her?"

"Whoa. Give me a break. It's only the morning after. . . ."

"I think she knows . . ."

Luke's tone suddenly changed to serious. "How?"

"Lucy guessed. It was bound to come out. . . ."

I heard Luke sigh heavily at the other end. "Okay. Right. Okay. Now calm down, T. J."

"Calm *down*?! She said she knew all about it. She said that you said I had a crush on you and you wanted to reassure her that it was all in my head. What's *that* all about?"

Luke was silent for a few moments. "Oh, that. Yeah. Listen, T. J. I was, er . . . testing the water to see how she'd react. Look. Let me handle this my own way. I need time to think. Um. Yeah."

"*Is* it all in my head?"

"You tell me, T. J."

"Oh, *please* don't start with all that again. What about last night?"

I could hear Luke sigh again. "Don't start getting all heavy on me. It was a kiss. One kiss. No big deal."

No big *deal*? I thought. How could he *say* that? A kiss that lasted almost three hours and now threatened to end my friendship with two of my best mates and had already ended my relationship with Steve. My mind was reeling, and I was at a loss as to what to say next.

"Look, got to go," said Luke. "Keep your chin up. I'll sort it."

"No, *no*, don't go," I blustered. "I need to know where I stand."

Next to me, I heard Izzie take a sharp intake of breath and shake her head. I knew I'd broken the golden rule of "Thou shalt always be cool" and crossed into sounding desperate. I didn't care.

"Where you stand?" said Luke lightly. "I don't know. Where are you?"

"In the classroom at school."

"Well, that's where you stand then," he said, then laughed. "Unless you're sitting, that is."

I didn't say anything. How could he be making jokes at a time like this? I thought.

"Hey, T. J.," said Luke. "Lighten up. Don't be so heavy. I'll sort it and be in touch."

And then he hung up. Izzie was looking at me with concern as I clicked my phone off and burst into tears.

Cures for Snog Rash

Add two to three drops of rose, camomile, or both, to a bowl of warm water. Soak a face towel in the water, then apply to the snog-rash area for a few minutes.

Alternatively, add a few drops of the same oils to your moisturizer and apply to the area.

Chapter 17

Fairweather Friends

The rest of the morning felt like eternity. I was dying to know if Nesta had spoken to Luke and what he'd said to her, but no way could I ask as she kept well out of my way, and Lucy avoided Izzie and me like we were the plague. Nesta looked as if she'd been crying, and it was all because of me. I felt so mean. And I felt sorry for Izzie, as she hadn't done anything.

"I am sooooo sorry," I said in the lunch break as Izzie and I sat by a radiator in the school hall. We both had sandwiches in front of us, but neither of us had any appetite. "None of this is your fault, and now it looks like Lucy's mad with you as well."

"Well, I'm mad with her now," said Izzie. "I mean, what is her problem? She's my oldest mate, and she hasn't even *tried* to see things from my angle *or* yours. She just stomped off with Nesta, and she hasn't given either of us a chance to explain anything. Some friendship, huh? It's like we're fairweather friends, pals if everything is hunky-dory. Friends are supposed to talk about things, weather the storms. Be friends, come what may. Resolve problems. Not first sign of trouble and ooh, we're not talking to you. It's pathetic. And now I'm mad. And by the looks that Lucy's been giving us all morning, she is too."

"I guess she's feeling protective of Steve and Nesta. I feel awful. Nesta looks really upset. She's been let down by two people, me and Luke."

Izzie sighed. "I know it must be tough for her. But it wasn't as if you went out of your way to get Luke. He's the one that should be feeling sorry. From everything you've told me, you've tried to resist."

"I did. I really did. I wish she'd let me explain. Anyway, it's all been an almighty waste of time. Looks like I've lost two of my best mates and finished with Steve and what for? One night with Luke and only a raw chin to show for it. Luke couldn't give a stuff about me. He was so weird on the phone, saying it was only a kiss and not to get heavy."

"I'd like to show him heavy," said Izzie. "I'd like to knock some sense into him. And so should you, T. J. I mean, come on, the guy's been using the same line on you and Nesta and who knows how many others? He ought to take responsibility for his actions. And his words. But boys can be cowards sometimes, and they *all* hate confrontation. It probably all came as a bit of a shock to him when you phoned. When they're under attack, some boys' first defense is to attack back. And who knows where he was when you called? You might not have got him on his own. If there were other boys around, he might have acted all cool because they were listening in. . . . You know, keep up the macho, I'm-so-cool image. Pathetic."

I glanced over at the other side of the hall, where Lucy and Nesta were huddled together with their backs to everyone else.

"It's not Luke I care about right now," I said. "It's Nesta and Lucy. I really value their friendship."

"And I thought that they valued ours," said Izzie looking over at them. "This is ridiculous."

"You don't have to sit with me if you want to go over."

"I know," said Izzie. "I *want* to sit with you. I'll speak to them when I'm good and ready."

"I wish I could make it all right."

"I think you should give Luke a piece of your mind. I think he's been getting away with murder. When's your next project meeting?"

"Tonight."

"Are you going to go?"

"Dunno."

During English in the afternoon, instead of working on the essay that Mr. Johnson had set us, I wrote a letter.

Dear Sian, Olivia, and Luke,

I'm really sorry, but I can't come to the meetings for the project anymore. It's due to circumstances beyond my control as some problems have come up that I have to deal with. I hope that you'll understand, and I really am sorry. I won't let you down, though, and will make sure that all the parts of the projects that I was doing get to you in time for the presentation. I've almost finished everything; it's just that I can't come to the meetings.

Best of luck with it all,
T. J.

As soon as school had finished, I raced out to the prefab and left the letter on the desk, where one of them would see it. Then I ran to the bus stop, praying that I wouldn't bump into one of them on their way in. I stood at the bus stop with my coat collar pulled up as far as it would go and my hair swept over my face in the hope that no one would see me.

Unfortunately, as I waited, a car pulled up and Olivia got out.

"Hey, T. J.," she said. "What you doing here? Not coming to the meeting?"

I shook my head. "No, er . . . sorry, something's come up, but I have been working on the parts I said I would, and I'll get them to you in time."

"Okay, cool," she said. "Is Sian in there already?"

"Um, don't think so. Why?"

Olivia shrugged. "Oh, no reason specially. How's your mate, Nesta?"

Omigod, does she know? I asked myself as panic flooded through me. But how could she?

"Um, Nesta's fine. Er . . . why do you ask?" I didn't want to say anything about her not speaking to me, as I intended to make things right with her if it was the last thing I did.

Olivia shifted uncomfortably. "I . . . I don't know if I should tell you, but . . . see, I've met Nesta, and I like her and well . . . I just wonder if one of us should warn her. . . ."

My sense of panic was replaced by a sense of dread. "Warn her about what?"

"About Luke. Remember I told you that he's a mate of my brother?"

"Yeah."

"Is Nesta really keen on him?"

"I . . . yes, she is, was, is. Why?"

"I think Luke's ready to do his usual act. He's met someone new, and Nesta's had her allotted time. . . ."

"Really? Er . . . someone new? Who?"

"Not certain, but I have an idea. He told William that he's really fallen in love this time. Poor girl, I say, as he only ever feels that way for about three months tops. Anyway, looks like Nesta might get dumped."

I wondered if she knew anything about Luke and me, but was playing it cool. "But why tell me?" I asked.

"Well, I thought he might have talked to you. You know, about Sian . . ."

"Sian?"

"Yeah. Well it must be her, mustn't it? Who else? I know she's not his usual type, but she did let it slip the other night that something had happened between them. I must say I was a bit surprised, but Luke must see something in her. I wasn't sure whether to say anything, but I know that Nesta's a mate of yours and well . . . looks like she might get hurt. I've known Luke for a long time, remember I told you . . ."

I nodded. "About his cut-off date. Looks like Nesta's not even going to make the three months."

"Yeah. He knows he's got her, so needs to make a new conquest. I think he's still trying to prove that he is Mister Attractive and can make anyone fall in love with him."

"So Nesta was just another conquest?"

"It's probably not that cold. I think he genuinely

does fall for the girls he goes out with, but then he meets someone new and can't resist seeing if he can get them as well. That's when it all gets messy, as he isn't very good about coming clean that he's moved on, and he leaves a trail of girls wondering where they stand with him. Bit of a coward when it comes to confrontation."

And in the meantime, he doesn't realize the damage he does, I thought. The friendships he can destroy. Well, he's not going to destroy mine just to prove something to himself.

"I know it should be Luke that tells Nesta," said Olivia, "but, knowing him from the past, he'll avoid the situation, so you can tell her if you want. Warn her so that she's ready for it. Anyway, better get going. See you next time."

As she walked off, I felt more confused than ever. Was Luke still involved with Sian, or could this girl that Luke was smitten over be me? Or someone else entirely? Not that I wanted to have a relationship with him anymore. No way. Losing my mates was too high a price to pay for a flaky relationship with a boy who didn't know what or who he wanted. I just wanted to find out what had been going on. As I stood there lost in my thoughts, I saw Luke appear around the corner and stride toward the school. My heart started beating in my chest. Maybe he'd come early in the hope of catching me on my own before

Sian and Olivia arrived from their schools, I thought. Or maybe he wanted to speak to Sian? No, no, I told myself, he'd reassured me many times that there was nothing going on with Sian, and I believed him. Maybe I shouldn't run away like a coward. Maybe I should talk to him and find out what was going on. Yes. He might be scared of confrontation, but I wasn't. I wanted to get my friends back, so I needed to be clear about what had been going on before I spoke to them again. I stepped out of the bus queue and started to walk toward him. As soon as he saw me, he veered off to the right, then called to a girl from Year Ten who had just come out of the school gates.

I couldn't believe it. He had *blanked* me. I felt myself crumble inside. Luckily my bus came round the corner a moment later, so I hastily rejoined the bus queue, dived onto the bus, and sat there in a daze for the journey home. When I got back, I told Mum that I didn't feel well, didn't want any supper, and was going straight to bed.

Once underneath my duvet, I tried to make sense of what had happened. Why had he turned away from me like he hadn't seen me? Surely he'd have been expecting me to have been at the meeting, so why blank me in the street? Should I call him, have it out with him? I wondered. But the courage I'd felt earlier seemed to have faded, and I felt weary of the whole business. Anyway, I told myself, he'd only tell me not to get heavy again. He said he'd sort it. Maybe I should let him. He'd probably call sooner or later, and when he did, I'd have my questions ready. I looked at the phone and willed it to ring. But then, he'd be in the meeting with Olivia and Sian. Or maybe he had a letter like mine to deliver, saying he wouldn't be coming to meetings either. I hoped not. What a mess. It would be a shame to blow the project after all the work we'd put in. Maybe I should call Nesta. She was probably at home in a similar state to me. Questioning everything. I felt awful about that. Maybe she was slagging me off to anybody who'd listen. My stomach knotted as I imagined her talking to Tony or with Lucy at her house, talking to her brothers and all of them hating me. How could I ever be friends with them again? They'd never let me. All of them would think I was a horrible person and maybe I was. A boyfriend stealer. And not just any boyfriend. I stole one of my best friends' boyfriend. Nesta was so brilliant when Hannah went out to South Africa last year, and I felt like I didn't have a friend in the world. She'd gone out of her way to make me feel welcome in her home and her life, and how had I returned her friendship?

Oh God. I hate myself. I should have resisted Luke last night. Told him to go home. *Why* didn't I? Because I am the worst person in the whole world. Yes, they are probably all sitting round right now talking about what a rotten person I am. And Luke?

Who knows what's going on in his mind. I'd been a complete fool? *Why* had I let him in last night? But after our marathon snogging session, I'd been so sure that he'd felt as strongly about me as I did about him and now, now I didn't know what to think. Am I desperate to have given in so easily? But it hadn't felt like that at the time; it had felt wonderful, perfect, meant to be. As the thoughts whirled round and round in my head, my mind began to feel exhausted. Is this what being in love is really like, I wondered as I recalled the conversation about it that I'd had with the girls only weeks ago. Feeling ill, like I wanted to curl up and die, and yet only last night I'd felt on top of the world, in heaven. Now I was in hell, hell, hell.

Not long after I'd taken to my bed, Mum came in with a thermometer. She put her hand on my forehead and looked at me anxiously. "Doesn't feel like you've got a temperature," she said as she held out the thermometer, "but pop this in your mouth and we'll see."

I didn't object. How could I tell her that I had heartache. The love bug. It might be internal, but it hurts just as bad as any physical illness. If only there was a tablet I could take to ease the pain, I thought, make it all go away. It's so easy with a cold or flu, you just take TheraFlu and have hot drinks. With a broken leg, you put on a bandage, but with a broken heart, what do you take? What can you do? There isn't an ointment or Band-Aid that can mend it.

After a few minutes, Mum took out the thermometer. "No, your temperature's normal, T. J. How are you feeling? What are the symptoms?"

I moaned and turned away from her to the wall. She was being so nice to me. If she only knew what a bad person I was. I felt tears in my eyes and didn't want her to see me crying.

"Sore head," I said. "Just need to sleep awhile."

"I'll bring you a paracetamol," said Mum, "then let me know if there's anything else you want."

"Thanks. Got to sleep now."

I waited for her to leave, but I could hear that she was still in my room. I could feel her looking at me even though my back was turned.

"T. J., is there anything you want to talk about? Anything bothering you?"

"No, just need to sleep," I said. All I wanted was to be left alone so that I could have a good cry.

"Is it the move to Devon that's upsetting you, because . . ."

"No. No, not that. I told you, I don't think I mind going now. In fact, I think it will be for the best."

Mum sat on the end of the bed and put her hand on my leg.

"So what then, love? You can tell me."

"I can't. Just . . . just have you . . . have you ever wished that you could turn back time?"

"Millions of times," said Mum softly. "Could it be . . . something to do with a boy?"

I felt tears well up in my eyes. "Yes. No . . . just . . . I've made such a huge mistake. . . ." I hesitated. I couldn't open up to her. I just couldn't. I felt too ashamed. She looked so worried, sitting there watching me that I felt I had to say something. "Oh don't worry, I'm not pregnant or on drugs or anything. It's just . . . a friend thing. I've . . . well, I messed up with my mates. But I'll . . . I'll sort it."

Mum squeezed my leg. "We all mess up from time to time, T. J. That's how we learn in life. It can be tough sometimes, but we can't always get it right. Thing is when you fall, you have two choices: to lie there feeling sorry for yourself, or to get up and try to right whatever you've done. No crime in falling. The only crime is staying down." She got up to go. "Nobody's perfect. Maybe you shouldn't be so hard on yourself. Whatever you've done, I'm sure there's a way to make it come right. Sleep on it. Things always seem better after a good night's sleep."

E-mail: Inbox (2)
From: <u>mwatts@fastmail.com</u>
To: <u>babewithbrains@psnet.co.uk</u>
Date: 12 December
Subject: Dresses

Hey, T. J.,

I picked up the dresses ready for us to try tomorrow. I hope you like yours. I think you will. It's not too girly.

See you soon.
Love,
Marie

E-mail: **Inbox (1)**
From: hannahnutter@fastmail.com
To: babewithbrains@psnet.co.uk
Date: 12 December
Subject: True Love

Hasta la bandango amigo,

Wow! Sounds like the real thing with Lukiemanukie. Please invite me to the wedding, and I will buy a hat. Can I be bridesmaid?

Your friend,
Hannah

From: <u>babewithbrains@psnet.co.uk</u>
To: <u>hannahnutter@fastmail.com</u>
Date: 12 December
Subject: Love Sucks

Dear Hannah,

No wedding. Except Marie's of course. No. No love affair either. It has all blown up in my face, and I have lost my friends and Steve. Feel the worst I've ever felt in my whole life (even worse than last time I felt my worst), and now I have to go and play happy bridesmaids as we're going to Devon for my dress fitting tomorrow. I think I will stand up in the church and yell "*Don't* do it." Love sucks. There ought to be a government warning against it. Will explain more later.

Lots of love,
T. J.

Chapter 18

I'm Going to Wash That Man Right Out of My Hair

The next day, I got up and ready to go to Devon, but when I got downstairs, Mum took one look at me and told me to go back to bed. I knew I looked bad, with bags under my eyes, which were still bloodshot from last night. I'd tried putting in some eye-drops that I'd found in the bathroom cabinet, but they hadn't helped much. I still looked like I'd been awake most of the night. Which I had.

"You look awful," she said. "How are you feeling?"

"Not one hundred percent, but I'll be okay."

"You might be coming down with something.

There's a lot of bugs around at the moment. My surgery is full of people with flu and coughs. Go back to bed for an hour or so as we're not leaving for Devon until midmorning. If you're still not feeling right, then, well, you'll just have to stay here."

I didn't argue. I was feeling rotten. I got back into bed and managed to doze off for half an hour until I was woken by my mobile. Panic seized me. What if it was Luke? Or Nesta?

"Hello?" I said tentatively.

It was Izzie. "Hey, how's it going?"

"Okay. Except Mum thinks I'm ill."

"Are you?"

"Not really, but I don't feel great. Have you spoken to Nesta and Lucy?"

"Lucy . . . sort of."

"What did she say?"

"Not a lot. I'm up at Costa in Highgate, as I'd arranged to meet her and Nesta here before this whole mad thing started. I thought that they might show up, but I doubt if they were still expecting me. Anyway, Lucy was waiting for Nesta, and we had a row. She accused me of taking sides. Can you believe it? Like she hasn't with Nesta. So I accused *her* of taking sides. Then she said something like, what do I expect and that I should have told them what was going on, but if I had . . . well, I'd have betrayed your trust, wouldn't I? What was I supposed to have done? I couldn't win whatever I'd done, either way I was going to upset one of you. Anyway, I said I'd promised not to tell, and you felt really bad about everything and she said, what, like, Nesta doesn't, as if I didn't care about Nesta's feelings at all. And that if we were all real mates and all trusted one another, then you or I would have let her and Nesta in on what was happening. And then she stormed off."

"Oh hell, I'm so sorry, Izzie. I should never have told you, then you wouldn't be in this mess."

"I'm glad you did. You had to tell someone, and I am your mate. And I understand why you didn't want to talk to Lucy or Nesta at the time."

"God, I wish I could turn the clock back, Izzie. Just a few days. Delete the tape. Rewind. I'm so sorry. I wish I could fix things."

"Seems to me that you have a choice. Luke, or Nesta and Lucy. It's not too late to fix it with them. But if you choose Luke, then I don't think Nesta and Lucy will stay friends with you. Least not for a while."

"I don't want Luke anymore, no way. No boy is worth losing your friends for. Anyway, I don't think Luke even wants to talk to me now. I wanted to have it out with him, but when I saw him after school yesterday, he blanked me."

"Ah," said Izzie. "But that could mean anything.

Remember when I told you that the defense of boys, who feel that they're under attack, is to attack back?"

"Yeah."

"Well, the ones that don't use that tactic do the ostrich routine. You know, stick their head in the sand. Try and ignore the whole situation and hope it goes away."

"So why was he coming to our school if he's trying to ignore things? He must have known he might bump into one of us."

"There you've got me stumped. I suppose he can't get out of the project meetings as he's coordinator, and the presentation is next week."

"So what are you going to do now?"

"Wait for Nesta," said Izzie. "I refuse to play the we're-not-speaking game. We've been mates for too long. And despite what Lucy may think, I do care about Nesta's feelings. I think you should call her, too. Don't give up."

After she'd hung up, I lay on my bed and stared at the ceiling. I'd been staring at it so much in the last few weeks, I knew it intimately, every crack, every lick of paint. My choice, Izzie had said. My choice. My friendship with the girls, or Luke? Luke, who I wasn't even sure of. Luke who, according to Olivia, had a cut-off date with all his girlfriends. There was no contest. We might have had an amazing night on

Thursday, but it had come at too high a price, and I wanted my friends back.

I took a deep breath and called Nesta's number. I got her voicemail so left a message asking her to call me.

Half an hour later, Izzie phoned again.

"I'm in the ladies' room," she whispered, "so I can't speak for long. Bad news I'm afraid. Nesta arrived, and I talked to her and tried to tell her that none of it was your fault and . . ."

"And?"

"And she's pretty cool. She's not mad with me like Lucy is. But she saw Luke last night after school, and he didn't say anything about finishing with her. She says he still wants to see her and that she means a lot to him. Can you believe it? He's such a rat. In fact, he's coming to meet her here later."

"Did she say anything about me?"

Izzie was quiet at her end of the phone.

"Please, Izzie, even if it's bad. I need to know."

"She said something about Luke saying that you got him when his guard was down, and you sort of threw yourself at him."

"What?" I felt my stomach churn. "That's what he told me when I confronted him about Sian. Said she'd kissed him, and he hadn't really wanted to kiss her back, but she threw herself at him. And Nesta believed him about me, huh?"

"Think so. I *am* sorry, T. J. I know you really thought he was The One."

"Yeah, me and a long list of idiots by the sound of it," I said. "Does Nesta hate me?"

"Er . . . well, let's just say that you're not up there with her favorite people right now."

"Someone's got to tell her what Luke is really like, Izzie. I tried to call her but got her voicemail."

"Do you want me to have another go?"

"You can try, but I think it's best if it comes from me. Are you going to stay and see Luke?"

"No way. I'd punch him if I saw him. I think he's a creep. He's playing both of you along in my opinion."

After she'd hung up, I went and took a bath. It was like I wanted to wash the whole thing away. While I was lying there soaking, I could hear one of Dad's favorite CDs playing downstairs. It's the soundtrack to the film *South Pacific*. There's a track that goes, "I'm going to wash that man right out of my hair." Too right, I thought as I reached for the shampoo.

The journey down to Devon took just under four hours, and Mum tucked me up in the back under a blanket, so I managed to doze off for a while. The rest of the time I just watched the fields flash by. I thought about what Izzie had told me, and I felt myself getting angrier and angrier. How could Luke have lied about me to Nesta? I wondered if he had a clue about the pain and confusion he was causing. I knew it was going to be hard, but I had to talk to Nesta and somehow get through to her that her boyfriend was a liar.

We arrived late afternoon and went straight to the cottage that Marie and Stuart had bought. It was a quaint little place, but in a mess as they'd only recently moved in and loads of stuff was still in boxes. Mum got busy straight away, putting the rubber gloves on and starting to clean out cupboards in the kitchen while Dad went to check out the garden and a dilapidated old greenhouse, which was great because it gave me some time alone with Marie. Even though she's a lot older than me, I've always found her easy to talk to.

"How you feeling?" she asked as we took mugs of tea into her bedroom. "Mum said you've been under the weather."

"Sort of."

"Flu bug?"

"Not really."

"Boy trouble?"

"How did you guess?"

Marie smiled. "I know the symptoms. Listless. Sad, bloodshot eyes. Look like the weight of the whole world is on your shoulders. Going to tell me about it?"

"Not much to tell. Only that I've ruined my life, lost my friends, hurt a really nice boy, and been let down by the only boy I ever loved, or thought I loved."

"Oh. So nothing major then?" she joked.

I gave her a weak smile. "How did you know that Stuart was The One, Marie?"

She sat on the bed and took a sip of her tea. "Oh God. Loads of reasons. He makes me laugh. I love being with him. I can't imagine life without him."

"Yeah, but how do you really know that he's The One?"

"He just is. It feels right. It's different to being with anyone else. I know that he's there for me. He'd do anything for me, and I feel the same about him. Already he's like family in that I know he's a hundred percent on my side. I trust him completely."

When she said the bit about trust, I felt my eyes watering.

"Hey," said Marie. "It can't be that bad. Are you going to tell me about it?"

"Promise you won't hate me?" I asked.

"Never," she said, taking my hand and holding it as I filled her in on the whole story. When I'd finished she looked at me kindly. "My poor T. J. Sounds like you need to talk to this boy. And to Nesta. Get a few things straight."

I shook my head. "Can't. Everybody hates me except Izzie. Nesta's not speaking to me, and Izzie thinks that Luke is doing the ostrich routine. You know, head in the sand."

"Then get him to take his head *out* of the sand. Talk to him. Ask him what the hell he thinks he's playing at."

"I tried after school last night, and he blanked me. It was awful. Anyway, what is there to say? When I tried to talk to him before, he told me not to get heavy and said that I was being demanding."

"Well, if he already thinks you are, and knowing you as I do, I can't imagine it as you're not a demanding kind of person, but if he *thinks* you are, then you've got nothing to lose. You want your mates back, so sort it with him. Be demanding. Ask him what his game is. If a boy has any respect for your feelings, he will give you the time, listen to how you are. Your feelings are as important as everyone else's in all of this, and you've had a rough ride by the sound of it. I know people have gotten hurt, but so have you and you matter as well. Call Nesta. And call him." She pointed to the phone by the bed, then got up to go. "No time like the present. I'll keep the wrinklies busy and make sure no one comes in."

I suppose I didn't look convinced as Marie turned back to me when she got to the door. "*Do* it," she urged. "You can't spend all weekend not knowing what's going on. Phone them."

After she'd gone, I sat and stared at the phone for

a few moments, then I picked up the receiver and dialed Nesta's number.

It was still switched off so, once again, I left a message.

Next I dialed Luke's number. He answered immediately.

"Hey, Watts," he said. "I was just thinking about you. We got your letter about not coming to the meeting. What's that all about?"

He sounded so cheerful it took me by surprise. How could he sound so happy when I was in torment? I asked myself.

"Why did you blank me yesterday?"

"Oh *that*? I wanted to talk to you, but Nesta was about ten yards behind you. You had your back to her so you couldn't see her. I didn't want her to see us together. I didn't want to hurt her more than necessary . . ."

But it's okay to hurt me, I thought. "So you did a runner?"

"*No*. Not exactly. In fact, when you'd got on the bus, I went and spoke to her. She was pretty mad with me."

I decided to confront him about everything. Marie was right, I had nothing to lose. "Yeah, so you told her that I threw myself at you. You *know* it wasn't like that."

"I most certainly do," said Luke in a low voice. "It was fantastic."

"So *why* did you lie?"

Luke sighed into the phone. "Oh, come on, T. J. Do we *have* to do this?"

"Yes. We *do*. I need to know what's going on. Izzie told me that you and Nesta are still an item. I thought you said that you were going to finish with her?"

"I am. I will, but I need to do it in my own time. I like Nesta, and as I said, I don't want to hurt her. Everything was happening a bit fast, so I thought I'd carry on seeing her for a while and let her down slowly."

I couldn't believe that he was still keeping it up and, for a moment, was lost for words.

"T. J., you still there?" asked Luke.

"Yes."

"Let's meet up next week. I really want to see you," he said, making his voice go husky again. "I've been thinking about you and Thursday night a lot. I can't wait . . ."

I could hear footsteps outside the door. "Look, got to go. Bye, Luke."

It was Marie. She put her head round the door. "I've brought you something to soothe your eyes," she said, holding two slices of cucumber out to me. "Everything okay?"

I wanted to scream. "*Nooooooo*. Not all right. I can't believe it. He still wants to see me. Says he's been *thinking* about me. Says he wants to let Nesta down slowly, and he'll finish with her in his own time."

Marie came and sat by me on the bed. "Hmm. *That's* a familiar story. Do you really, really care for this boy?"

"I . . . I don't think so. No, I can't. It's a mess. It all feels way too complicated, and I don't want to lose my friends over him."

"Then tell him," said Marie, "and them."

"What did you mean just now, it's a familiar story?"

Marie got up and made sure that the door was firmly closed. "Promise you won't tell Mum or Dad?"

"Promise."

Marie sat on the bed. "When you asked me before how I knew Stuart was The One and I said trust, well, that's a lesson I had to learn the hard way."

"How come?"

"Remember I was seeing a guy called Matthew for a while?"

I nodded. "Vaguely. A couple of years ago? Doctor at the hospital where you worked in Bristol? I never met him though because you never brought him home."

"Well, there was a reason for that," said Marie. "See, what I didn't ever tell any of you is that he was married. That's why I said familiar story. I was such an idiot, T. J., talk about naive. He told me that he and his wife were unhappily married and that they were going to split up, and they had no relationship to speak of anymore and me, like a total fool, believed every word of it. He was always telling me that I was the great love of his life and that he would leave her in his own time as he didn't want to hurt her more than necessary et cetera, et cetera . . ."

"I never knew."

Marie looked at the door. "Nobody did. But at the time, it felt so right, I thought I really loved him. It was the real thing, and he would leave his wife for me. . . ."

"So what happened?"

"One day, I was asked to stand in for a colleague on the prenatal clinic and guess who was in the class? His wife. His five months' pregnant, very sweet wife. So much for their relationship being over. When I asked him about it, he said it was just one night, and he still intended to leave her after the baby was born. I could tell from meeting her that she didn't have a clue, and she was looking forward to the birth of her child."

"I'm so sorry, Marie. You must have been gutted."

"I was. Heartbroken, and I felt like such a cow. I wouldn't have got involved if I hadn't thought his marriage was as good as over. He made his wife out to be this unfeeling monster, but she was a lovely woman. But he made me realize that if he was stringing his wife along, at a time when she needed him most and telling lies behind her back, then he might do the same thing to me. It made me realize that the most important thing in any relationship is trust. Oh, I know it's different with you, T. J. You're much younger, and I'm sure that this Luke is nothing like Matthew, but I just wanted to warn you that there are men out there like that, and what Luke is doing to Nesta, he may well do to you. It sounds to me like Luke doesn't know what he wants; either that or he's a coward like Matthew was."

"So what happened to Matthew?"

"Still with his wife last I heard. I finished with him as soon as I realized that he was lying to me, but it took me a long time to get over it. I felt awful. Evil. I kept seeing his wife in my mind, and I felt so mean."

"I know. That's how I felt when I saw how upset Nesta was, when she realized that Luke had cheated on her with me. But now he's talked her round again and instead of being mad with him, she thinks I threw myself at him, and she's mad with me."

"Is he worth it, T. J.?"

I shook my head. "Absolutely not. No way am I going to give up two of my best friends for someone who, a few months down the line, might decide that some other unsuspecting victim is the love of his life, and I'll find myself on the scrap heap."

"Exactly," said Marie. "But the bottom line is, do you trust him?"

I shook my head. "Not anymore."

"Do you trust Nesta?"

I nodded. "One hundred percent. She couldn't lie or keep a secret if she tried."

"Then there's your answer," said Marie getting up, going to the wardrobe, and pulling out two stunning dove-gray dresses with tiny white snowflakes embroidered round the hem. "But in the meantime we've got a wedding coming up, so let's forget about Luke for a while and try these dresses on!"

Aids for Bloodshot or Tired Eyes

1) Soak two camomile tea bags in hot water. When the water has cooled, squeeze the tea bags out, lie back, and apply the bags to your eyes.
2) Cut two thin slices of cucumber. Lie back and apply to the eyes.

Chapter 19

Confrontations

"Hi, can I speak to Nesta?" I asked.

It was Saturday night, and Mum and Dad were finishing supper with Marie and Stuart in the kitchen. I hadn't much appetite, so I'd excused myself and made a beeline for the phone in Marie's bedroom. All I wanted to do was get on the phone and get my friends back.

"Hold on, I'll just go and call her," said Tony, who had picked up the phone. He came back a few minutes later. "She says she's not in."

Next I tried Lucy. Her mobile was on voicemail, so I left a quick message saying that I needed to talk to her. Then I called Izzie. Luckily she was there, so I filled her in on my latest phone call with Luke.

"I told you so," she said. "He's telling you one thing and Nesta another."

"I'm going to tell Nesta," I said. "That is, if I can get to speak to her."

"And I'll tell Lucy," said Izzie. "That is, if I can get to speak to her. I'm going over there tomorrow, and I'm going to sit in the front porch if she doesn't let me in."

"Maybe I'll come and join you depending on what time we get back. I could bring a banner saying 'Sorry.'"

On Sunday we didn't get away as early as I'd hoped in the morning, as Dad wanted to check out estate agents, and Marie and Mum still had wedding plans to go through. I went with Dad to look in estate agents' windows. It might have been my imagination, but he didn't seem as enthusiastic as he had been in the beginning, and it was me who seemed the more eager of the two of us, although I was beginning to regret having told Mum that I was happy to move. On the one hand, it would be a new start for me—a new chapter was just what I wanted after I'd put the record straight with Lucy and Nesta. Down here, no one would know me or what I'd done. On the other hand, if I could make things right with my mates, the last thing I'd want to do was leave them.

After a lunch of Marie's spaghetti bolognese (it's her speciality, and the only thing she can cook. I wondered if Stuart's realized yet that unless he cooks, he's destined to eat takeout or the same meal for the rest of eternity), everyone wanted to do some Christmas shopping in a market that was held in the local scout hut. I saw loads of things there that were perfect for presents for Nesta and Izzie and Lucy. As we browsed and I bought a few items (including a recipe book for Marie), I thought I couldn't imagine life without the girls even after we'd moved to Devon. I would always think of Izzie when I saw a crystal or aromatherapy kit. Glittery makeup and bath gels would always remind me of Nesta, and any romantic type of fashion or lovely fabric would always make me think of Lucy and her passion for design. I felt sad as I bought them presents, thinking that this might be our last Christmas in the same city. I couldn't bear to think it might all end on a sour note. I bought a silver and amethyst bracelet for Izzie, a red velvet scarf for Lucy, and a tiny handbag with a fluffy trimming for Nesta. I hoped that they'd accept my gifts and still be my friends, and we could spend the coming holiday together as we'd planned before this whole fiasco with Luke had started. I'd made up my mind, Luke was history. I just hoped that Lucy, Izzie, and Nesta would be a part of my future no matter where I lived.

I made sure that I got to school early on Monday morning and was waiting at the gates to catch Nesta and Lucy on their way in.

Lucy was the first to arrive. She looked confused when she saw me as if she didn't know how to react.

"Lucy," I called. "Can I speak to you?"

She hesitated for a moment, then came over.

"I wanted to say that I'm really, really sorry," I blurted. "I never meant for any of this to happen and want you to know, *please* will you be my friend again? I'll do anything, and I know I've messed up badly and handled everything the wrong way. But it's all over with Luke and me. I promise. I've been such a fool."

Lucy looked embarrassed. "I saw Izzie yesterday. She came over and wouldn't leave until she'd told me everything."

I smiled. "Did she set up camp on your front porch?"

Lucy smiled back. "Something like that. She said she wasn't going until we'd talked everything through and that she'd brought sandwiches and a sleeping bag and was going to sleep in the shed if I didn't let her in. Anyway, she told me everything about you and Luke and everything that's happened, and . . . and . . . I guess I was a little hasty in judging you."

"Does that mean we can be friends again? I know it's only been a short while, but it's felt like an eternity. I've missed you so much, and it's been hell not being able to talk to you."

Lucy nodded. "I've missed you, too—like this weekend, it felt like something wasn't right. But . . . look, T. J., I do want to be friends, but let's get one thing straight: Friends put each other first and tell each other everything. You should have said something about fancying Luke."

I nodded. "I know. I really, *really* know, but . . . I was afraid that you'd hate me."

"I don't hate you. You can't help who you fancy, but you can help what you do about it."

"I know, and nothing like this will *ever* happen again. I promise that from now on I will tell you everything, *everything*. . . ."

"Deal," said Lucy, smiling.

I wrapped my arms around her and gave her a huge hug. "I really, honestly, truly didn't mean it to happen," I said. "I've been *sooo* stupid . . . and unhappy. . . ."

"I guess love makes us all a bit stupid sometimes. . . ."

"It's made me realize a lot. . . ."

Just at that moment, Nesta came round the corner. She looked taken aback to see me being so pally with Lucy and turned to walk the other way.

"Nesta," I called after her.

"Later," she said as she walked off toward the assembly hall.

It wasn't going to be easy winning Nesta back, I thought.

"Any ideas?" I asked Lucy.

"Groveling might work," she replied. "If that doesn't work, try bribery, a lifetime's supply of chocolate or something. And I'll try and talk to her in the break."

At break, Lucy made a beeline for Nesta as she headed out of class, and I prayed that she might get through to her. However, when we went back into class fifteen minutes later, Lucy looked over at me and shook her head.

"I'll try at lunch," said Izzie. "If nothing else, she has to realize what Luke is really like."

"Thanks, Iz," I said. "But I think it should come from me."

"Well, let's just hope she doesn't shoot the messenger," said Izzie with a grim look, "or try to strangle you. But then again, it might give us a chance to practice our first-aid skills."

I lightly punched her arm. Thank God for Izzie, I thought. She's kept me sane through all this.

At lunch, I was first out ready to confront Nesta. As she came out of the classroom, she saw that I was waiting and headed in the other direction. Lucy and Izzie came out soon after and gave me a nod to go after her, so I followed and caught up with her.

"Nesta," I said. "We have to talk."

"Nothing to say," she said.

"It's about Luke. . . ."

"I *said* nothing to say. He told me about how you threw yourself at him." Then she stopped and turned to me. "How could you, T. J.?"

I took a deep breath. "I'm sorry, Nesta. I really am. But it wasn't how he said it was."

She waved her hand as if dismissing what I was saying. "Yeah, yeah. Whatever."

"No. *No*. Nesta. Not whatever. It wasn't all in my head, you have to believe that. Luke has been lying to both of us."

She shook her head. "You just don't get it, do you?" she asked. "He's into me. End of story. Now get your own boyfriend." And she started to walk off down the corridor.

I couldn't let her go off like that. It was going to be the hardest thing I'd ever done, and I knew it would hurt her, but she had to know the truth. "I spoke to him after he'd told you that story about me throwing myself at him and . . ."

I saw her slow down, so I caught up with her again. "Listen, Nesta, I'm really sorry to have to tell you this and . . . and . . . I'm sure Luke *does* like you. He told me that he likes you, but he's also told me that he's going to finish with you."

Nesta stopped. She didn't look at me, but I could see that she was listening.

"He . . . he said he wants to be with me and doesn't want to hurt you, so he's going to go out with you a bit longer and let you down slowly. I don't even know if that's true, but I think you ought to know what he's saying behind your back."

Nesta didn't say anything.

"I'm really, really sorry. And I didn't throw myself at him, honestly. There was one time when we kissed. *One* time . . . and it wasn't me forcing myself on him. It really wasn't. He was with me for three hours. . . ."

Nesta finally looked me in the face. Her expression was one of anger and hurt. "He told *you* that he's going to finish with *me*?"

"Yes. Can't you see what he's doing, Nesta? He's telling us both different things . . ."

"And . . . when he kissed you, he was with you for three hours?"

I nodded.

Nesta ran her fingers through her hair and looked agitated. "Okay. Okay . . . Let me get my head round this. So you're saying that Luke lied to me about you?"

"Yes. Remember my snog rash?"

"I asked him about that, and he said that Steve must have given you that."

"No way. And anyway, you've seen Steve. He hardly has to shave. I know it's hard to hear, but it was Luke."

"And you say that he's planning to dump me?"

"That's what he said."

"Okay. Okay. So . . . if he *does* dump me, are you going to go out with him?"

"*Noooo*. No way. I can't trust him. Neither can you. That's why I'm telling you all this. But you *can* trust me, Nesta. I'm being totally honest with you now. I don't think we're the only girls he's stringing along either. Sian thinks he wants to be with her as well."

"Sian? That blond girl?"

"Yes. He told me that he didn't fancy her. Not his type he said, but then she told me that he'd kissed her and when I confronted him about it, he gave me the line he gave you about me. That she threw herself at him."

Nesta looked shocked. "Sian? I can't believe it."

"Well, who knows what's really going on in her head, but I don't think it's entirely her fault that she thought she stood a chance with him. He can't bear to tell anyone the truth. I think he wants to know that he can have all of us. But I've had enough of him. I don't want any more misunderstandings, not knowing what's going on. I want to be with people who are totally on the level, who I can trust and who trust me. I want us to be friends again more than anything in the world."

Nesta gave me a long hard cold stare. "I'll kill him," she said then turned and walked away.

I stared after her, wondering if I should follow her, when Izzie came up behind me. "Leave her," she said. "She probably needs to be on her own for a while."

E-mail: **Outbox (1)**
From: <u>babewithbrains@psnet.co.uk</u>
To: <u>hannahnutter@fastmail.com</u>
Date: 15 December
Subject: Love

Dear Hannah,

God, I miss you. So much has been happening here, and I've learned so much—mainly that the most important thing in any relationship is trust. I really liked Luke a lot, but I can't trust him, not like I can my friends. I really hope I can win them back.

Love,
T. J.

From: <u>hannahnutter@fastmail.com</u>
To: <u>babewithbrains@psnet.co.uk</u>
Date: 16 December
Subject: Love

Ma petite T. J.,

    Methinks you are very wise, and I just want you to know that even though we are many miles apart now I trust you completely. Friends are forever, and I shall pray from afar that they all see sense and make it up with you.

Love and stuff,
Hannahalulu

Chapter 20

Presentation

"He's just come in," said Izzie, coming over to the stand where I was busy with Olivia pinning up our work for the project. It was the afternoon of the presentation, and anyone involved had been let out of school for the afternoon to go to the Institute in Highgate to prepare for the evening. The hall was buzzing with teachers and pupils rushing about, making last minute adjustments, all busy trying to show their work to its best advantage in its own screened-off area.

"Time to face the music, I guess," I said as I glanced over my shoulder and saw that Luke was heading straight for me.

"Let me know how it goes," said Izzie, and pointed

to the other side of the hall, "and I'm only just over there if you want me to come over and knock his lights out."

"What happened to your Buddhist philosophy about not harming any living creature?"

"I wouldn't *kill* him," she said with a grin, "only maim."

"Thanks, Iz," I said, then turned back to the board and began to pin up my poster detailing all the people who'd lived in Hampstead. Our area did look impressive. On one side were all the photographs that Steve had taken for me before we broke up, color blow-ups of the houses we'd visited. On the right were my posters of all the famous people who lived in the area, a map of where they'd lived, and Luke had picked a selection of quotes from the writers and photos of some of the paintings of the area. Sian had done some fabulous illustrations of streets, shops, and houses, and Olivia had done a great job on the layouts of all the tidbits of information in between. The whole effect was very professional and glossy.

"It's beginning to take shape," said Olivia, standing back as Luke came to join us. "I think it's going to look good. Don't you think, Luke?"

Luke looked at me and not the work. "Yeah. Looks great. Sorry I'm late. Er . . . Olivia," he said as he reached into his pocket and pulled out his car keys, "could you start getting the boxes from the trunk of my car. I've got a load of brochures on the houses that people can take away if they want. I need to just check a few things in here, then I'll come and help you unload."

"Sure," said Olivia, and headed off for the door.

I carried on pinning up the work.

"So why haven't you returned any of my phone calls?" asked Luke. "I've been going out of my mind."

"Oh, I think you know *exactly* why," I said, without turning to look at him.

"Actually I don't," he said. "I think we need to talk."

I couldn't resist. "Oh, do we have to do this now?" I asked.

"Yes. I need to know what's going on. . . ."

"Oh, don't get all heavy, Luke," I said, turning to him at last. "Tonight's the big night."

"You know I've finished with Nesta, don't you?"

"I know that Nesta finished with *you*," I said. "Lucy told me." Apparently she didn't waste any time and finished with him the same day that I'd spoken to her about his lying.

"So that means it won't be a problem with us anymore."

"Whadt?" I couldn't believe his cheek. "Er . . . reality check, Luke. I think there's a *major* problem with us, a few in fact. One, that you're a liar. Two, that

you seem to have some kind of problem being alone, and three, that I can't trust you. Oh. And four, I wouldn't go out with you if you were the last person on the planet."

Luke looked taken aback. "But . . . I thought we had something special."

"And so did Nesta, and so does Sian and God knows how many other idiots. Now, if you'll excuse me, I think I'll go and give Olivia a hand with those boxes."

At that moment, Sian came over and looked coyly at Luke. You're welcome to him, I thought as I made my way across the hall.

Izzie caught me up at the door. "Everything okay?"

"Sure. How about you? Is your stuff up and ready?"

Izzie nodded in the direction of her stand. She'd managed to get loads of posters of the leaders of all the different religions and a big statue of the laughing Buddha took pride of place on a table at the front and good old Steve had photographed all the churches in the area for her. She'd even persuaded Trevor to dress up as a swami although he didn't look too comfortable about it as people kept going past him singing "Hare Krishna."

Suddenly Izzie's eyes swiveled to the door. "Omigod," she said. "Major babe alert. Ding dong. Eyes left. Which school is that divine apparition from?"

I turned to where she was looking and saw that a tall boy had come in behind Olivia. He was striking, like he could have been Orlando Bloom's younger brother.

"Don't know but he's definitely a five star hubba hubba," I said as I checked him out. "Is Nesta here yet?"

"Down the end of the hall helping Lucy," said Izzie pointing to the far right of the hall, where Lucy was busy dressing a mannequin while Nesta gave instructions. Then Izzie laughed. "Looks like they've clocked boy babe as well."

I glanced over and saw that both Lucy and Nesta were looking in the boy's direction. Lucy saw us looking and gave us a wave. As we waved back, Nesta looked over, then turned away when she saw me.

"How is Nesta by the way?" I asked.

"She's been pretty quiet all week," said Izzie. "She still not speaking to you?"

"She did speak to me yesterday," I said, "when we came out of maths. Only to say that she'd never speak to me again though."

"Ah," said Izzie. "So there's hope then."

"How do you see that?"

"No one can ever say never. She said yesterday that she'd never look at another boy as long as she lived and look at her now. She's definitely checking the hubba hubba boy out. If she can break her vow never to look at another boy in the short time of twenty-four hours, she may come round to being mates with you again."

A few moments later, Lucy made her way through the throng to join us. "Hey, have you checked out the boy over there."

"Oh, yes," said Izzie. "Mucho tasty."

"That's what Nesta said," said Lucy. "I think she may be on the road to recovery."

Luke walked past on his way to the door and took one look at Lucy, Izzie, and I, then glanced down the hall at Nesta.

"Got to get some last-minute photocopying done." He gulped and disappeared fast.

For the next half hour, we kept busy with the preparations. I stayed away from Nesta. I felt that the ball was in her court, and there was nothing more I could say or do to win her back. In the meantime, Izzie came over to see me, then went to check on Nesta and Lucy. Then Lucy came over to me while Nesta watched from the fashion stand, and I watched her from the history stand. After about half an hour of this, I glanced over at her and caught her looking at me. She stuck her tongue out at me and made a silly face. Then she gave me a look with one eyebrow raised that was like a challenge—as if to say, what are you going to do about it? I pulled my worst face back at her. I'd perfected it in the mirror years ago. I put an index finger on my nose to make it snub, stretched the corners of my mouth out with the little fingers of both hands, stuck my tongue out and crossed my eyes.

Just at that moment, who walked by but hubba hubba boy? He stopped and stared at me. Behind him, I saw Nesta totally crease up laughing.

"Hmm. Very ladylike," said the boy.

"I do try," I said. "I've been told that it's a very seductive look."

The boy grinned. "Unforgettable," he said, then moved on.

"On the pull again, huh?" said a familiar voice a few moments later.

It was Nesta.

"Yeah, but I don't think he fell for my super sexy look," I said with a laugh.

"Slut," said Nesta. But she was smiling as she said it.

"I'm really, really sorry. . . ."

"Boooring," yawned Nesta. 'We've been there done the apologies and stand-offs. Look. Bottom line is, I miss you. And on top of that, Lucy and Izzie can't spend their lives going between us."

I held my breath for a moment. Was she making up?

"Okay. No more saying sorry, but you have to know that I know I've been totally out of order, but I would never ever have dreamed of doing what I did if I hadn't thought that Luke was really special.

Remember weeks ago, when we talked about soul-mates. I . . . I thought Luke was my soulmate. I know it sounds major stupid now that we know that he's such a liar, but . . . I had all the symptoms that Izzie described. Sick, stupid, ill, couldn't sleep, couldn't think straight. I did think it was a once in a lifetime thing."

Nesta didn't say anything for a few moments. "The One, huh?"

"Yeah. Bummer."

"Yeah. Major bummer."

For a moment I thought she was going to get mad at me for saying I thought Luke was my soulmate. I decided to change the subject. "So you were saying. Poor Lucy and Izzie. If we don't talk, it would be cruel to them."

"Yeah, why should they suffer when it's really Luke who's the rat-faced, pig-goat-poo person in all of this. Where is he, by the way?"

"Out the back somewhere. Keeping out of the way. Once we got the stand up, he made a load of excuses to disappear. I think being in the same room as both of us is difficult for him, never mind Lucy and Izzie glowering at him from their stands."

"Good," said Nesta. "If I never see him again, it will be too soon."

Lucy and Izzie came over. "Hey, you're talking."

"Yeah," said Nesta. "We thought we owed it to

you and Izzie. You're going to wear yourselves out going between the two of us, so for your sakes and *only* that, yes, we are going to make up. Okay, T. J.?"

"Double okay," I said.

"Excellent," said Lucy.

"Now, more importantly," said Nesta. "You guys may be stupid enough to believe in finding The One and doing your head in in the process but I, the only sensible person here, know better and that there are many Ones out there. So. Who's that boy babe cruising the hall?"

"I saw him first," said Izzie.

"No, I did," said Lucy as she gave Izzie a slight shove.

"T. J., you want to stake your claim before battle commences?" asked Nesta.

"Do you fancy him?" I asked Nesta.

"D'oh, *yeah*. Just what I need in my time of grief."

"Then he's yours," I said.

"Chicken," laughed Nesta. "Anyway, we don't even know who he is yet. But I intend to find out."

"I thought you were through with boys," said Izzie.

"Nope," said Nesta. "Just ones like Luke. There's plenty more fish in the sea and not *all* of them are razor sharks."

"Very wise," said Izzie. "And if at first you don't succeed . . ."

"Try, try, try again," Lucy finished for her.

"No," said Izzie. "If at first you don't succeed, sky-diving is not for you."

We all cracked up. Lucy looked at the three of us and grinned widely. "God, I'm so glad we're mates again. This last week has been hell. I'm so glad you managed to see things from T. J.'s angle, Nesta. . . ."

"Yeah," said Izzie. "She's had a tough time too, and there are two sides to every story."

"Or three if you're involved with Luke," said Nesta.

I was about to say four if you included Sian, but bit my lip.

"Yeah," said Izzie. "It's like that saying, before you criticize someone, walk a mile in their shoes."

"Oh very wise, Obi-Wan Kenobi," said Nesta. "But there's another bit to that saying. Before you criticize someone, walk a mile in their shoes. That way, when you do criticize them, you'll be a mile away, and you'll have their shoes."

We all laughed again. I felt great. Out of the corner of my eye, I saw Luke come back through the doors. He took one look at us and turned on his heel. I didn't care. In fact, I felt relieved he'd disappeared. I could hardly believe it. Here we all were, me, Izzie, Lucy, and Nesta together, having a laugh like we used to. There was only one more person I needed to make things right with and that was Steve.

I'd noticed him as soon as I'd arrived at the hall, he was up on the left busy arranging his photographs on his stand. He'd kept his head down the whole time as if he was in a world of his own. Lucy saw me looking in his direction.

"He's okay," she said. "He was cut up, but he'll be okay."

"I feel bad about him," I said, "really bad. He deserved better than the way I broke up with him."

"He'll get over it. Steve's not one to mooch about."

I winced inwardly as I thought about how he must have felt waking up, turning on his computer, and finding my message there. Like—good morning and you're dumped. Love, T. J. How could I have had such disregard for his feelings?

"There has to be some right way to finish with people," I said. "It's like I went to one extreme with my stupid e-mail charging in with my 'must be honest, right now' policy. And Luke went to the other extreme by avoiding confrontation and not telling anyone anything but what they wanted to hear. We both ended up hurting people. There has to be a middle way to do it."

"Apparently there are fifty ways to leave your lover." Lucy laughed, then began to sing the song "Fifty Ways to Leave Your Lover" by Paul Simon. I tried to muffle her as her voice got louder and louder.

I so wanted to go over and talk to Steve, go back to how we were, mates, having a laugh, because even though I didn't want to get back with him, I did miss his company. For a moment I understood why Luke found it so hard to end relationships. So maybe someone isn't the *great* love of your life, your soulmate, The One, but like with Steve, you still like them. You certainly wouldn't want to hurt them. You can love people in different ways, I thought, as Luke would say—on different levels. It's hard knowing that you're going to hurt someone or, in my case, *have* hurt someone. I guess for Luke not saying anything must have seemed like an easy option. But people still do get hurt, I reminded myself. It's damaging to string someone along under false pretences, giving them hope where there is none. It only prolongs the pain. But as I watched Steve, I thought, maybe Luke wasn't so much a rat as a coward. It's a biggie facing up to the responsibility that when you have a relationship with someone, and they really like you, you hold their heart in your hand. I don't want to be a coward. One day very soon, I'm going to call Steve and talk to him honestly about everything that's happened. I just hope that I can find the right words and that he'll still be my friend. Not boyfriend. Friend. Even though things hadn't worked out with Luke, I couldn't deny that what I'd felt on the night he came to my house had been really special. I wanted more of that lovely feeling of being hopelessly in love, but without the complications of people getting hurt and secrets and lies.

At six-thirty, everyone was ready and there was a hush of anticipation as Mrs. Allen showed Susan Barratt, the school governor, and Sam Denham, the journalist, around. The hall looked wonderful as some Year Eight pupils had dressed a huge Christmas tree on the stage, and the room smelled wonderfully festive with the delicious smell of cinnamon and clove coming from the mulled wine on the refreshments tables set up ready for the public.

Both Sam and Mrs. Barratt seemed very impressed and stopped to speak to just about everyone on all the stands, Sam spending a little longer on the fashion stand talking to Nesta. She looked well pleased and looked over at me and winked after he'd moved on. When Sam and Mrs. Barratt had done their rounds, the doors opened and in flooded everyone's friends and families.

Mum and Dad seemed genuinely interested in all of it, and after Dad had been round to look at all the stands, he came back and spent a long time studying ours.

"You love living here, don't you?" he asked as he looked at my map of Hampstead.

I nodded. "There's so much to do and see.

Remember that famous saying by Samuel Johnson: 'Tire of London and you're tired of life.'"

"He was right," said Dad. "This last few weeks, I've realized how much I love London too. I love to go to the concerts at the Barbican. I love to walk on the Heath. I love the theaters, the cinemas, the restaurants. It's all here on our doorsteps."

"So why are we moving, then?"

Dad smiled. "Good question. And one that I've been asking myself over and over these last few weeks. And so has your mother. So we've decided. We're not moving. Not just yet. We're not ready to give up our London lives yet. No. The new plan is that I still go part-time at the hospital and use my days off to enjoy London. We've lived here so long, but there's still so much we haven't done. Too busy working! I don't want to go to some quiet place and have nothing to do but potter in a greenhouse all day. Nope. We're staying put. So . . . how do you feel about that?"

I looked over at Nesta, Lucy, and Izzie. "How do I feel?" I gave him a big hug. "That's how I feel."

When Mum and Dad went over to get some mulled wine from the refreshments table, I noticed a couple who had just come in to the hall. With them was hubba hubba boy. I wasn't the only one who had seen them either because, as they made their way toward our stand, suddenly Nesta, Lucy, and Izzie all appeared beside me.

"Mine," said Lucy.

"No, mine," said Izzie.

"Nope, mine, mine, *mine*," insisted Nesta.

I laughed to see them jostling, when Olivia stepped out to greet the couple. "Hi, Mum, Dad," she said, then turned to me. "This is T. J., who's been working on the project with me."

"Hi," I said.

Then she turned toward hubba hubba boy. "And this is my brother, William."

I felt my jaw fall open.

"Another of your alluring looks," he said, smiling, as I shut my mouth.

"I have a whole range," I said as he moved behind me to join his parents, who were looking at Olivia's work. I quickly turned to the girls, who were all standing to the right of the screen. I pointed at the boy.

"Olivia's brother," I whispered. "Olivia's brother as in Luke's *best* friend."

"William?" asked Nesta.

I nodded.

"I heard Luke mention him, but we never met," she said.

The boy turned back and gave Nesta a long look.

"Contest over," said Lucy. "No doubt who *he's* interested in here."

Izzie cracked up laughing. "William as in Luke's

best friend. Cool." She nudged me to look over at the stage where Luke was sitting with Sian. He looked as if he was going to be sick. He caught my eye, and I felt an electric current run through me. There was such a sadness in his eyes as he looked at me and, for a brief moment, I felt a twinge of regret that things hadn't worked out differently. He'd said he thought we had something special. I think we did, but . . . how could I believe him? That's the trouble with liars, you can never know if they're telling the truth or spinning you a line. I made myself look away.

Nesta also glanced over at Luke, then turned back and fluttered her eyelashes in William's direction.

"Hmm," she said, smiling at us. "Luke's best friend. Now *this* could be very interesting."

Wedding Announcement

On Wednesday, December 24, Marie Watts
was married to Stuart Callaghan in Bigbury Bay,
Devon. Wedding guests traveled on a sea tractor to
Burgh Island Hotel, where they were snowed in for
several days due to unforeseen blizzards.
Bridesmaid T. J. Watts (15) said, "My parents
are delighted. My sister had a white wedding after all!"

SEE WHAT THE GIRLS ARE UP TO THIS TIME!
TURN THE PAGE FOR A SNEAK PEEK OF. . .

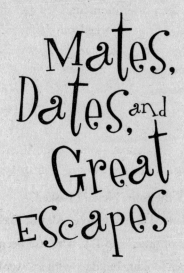

Mates,
Dates, and
Great
Escapes

by Cathy Hopkins
FROM SIMON PULSE

"What's the time, Nesta?" I asked.

She glanced at her watch. "Almost five."

"Loads of time," said T. J., who had been gazing up at a somber-looking building with a tower behind and to the right of the fountain. "Let's take a quick look in here." She got up and soon disappeared into a door.

Izzie, Nesta, and I wandered in after her and found ourselves in an elegant courtyard with pillars and stone steps leading upstairs.

T. J. consulted her guidebook. "This is the Palazzo Vecchio," she said. "It's where the Medici family lived in the fifteen hundreds."

"Shall we take a look upstairs?" I asked, pointing to the steps.

"You have to pay to go in, I think," said Nesta. She got out her purse and counted her euros.

"Still okay for time?" I asked.

Izzie glanced at her watch again. "Loads."

Nesta went over to the kiosk to enquire about entry. She turned back and gave us the thumbs-up. "Just got enough. Shall we do it?"

We nodded back at her.

Moments later we were up the stairs, exploring. The rooms were awesome, as all the walls and ceilings were covered with detailed paintings. Vast battle scenes in an enormous hall and seasonal country scenes in smaller rooms. There was something on every available surface and to see so much color and design packed into one area was breathtaking.

"Maybe this is what they did instead of using wallpaper," I said as we reached yet another painted room and gazed out of the window over Florence. "You know, you get a mate to come over and do a mural instead. It looks so ordinary from the outside, but inside they must have spent millions doing all this."

"Maybe we should do our rooms like this when

we get back," said Izzie. "You know, paint scenes from our lives. Maybe not. I don't think my mum would be too pleased if I painted a pic of you lot over her posh Sanderson wallpaper."

"She doesn't know what she's missing," I said. "I couldn't paint as well as this, but maybe I could see if any of Brandy Nelly's relatives are still alive and hire them to come over and do me a mural and a naked statue. Look lovely on the back patio with our garden homes and potted petunias."

T. J. gave me a look of despair. Sometimes I think she finds it hard that we don't all share her love of history.

From the window we could look out into the square, so I glanced over to the café to find Mrs. Elwes. I couldn't see her.

"Can't see the teachers," I said. "What time is it? Maybe we'd better get going."

"No," said Nesta. "We've only been in here about twenty minutes. We'll be fine."

"It's about half five," said Izzie.

"Is that all? I feel like we've been here ages," I said.

Suddenly T. J. slapped her forehead. "Ohmigod," she cried, then looked at her watch. "Time. Did any of you guys put your clocks forward when we got off the plane?"

We all shook our heads. Then it dawned on me. "Oh, no," I said. "No wonder time seemed to be lasting forever. We're still on English time. Italy is an hour ahead. Remember Mrs. Elwes told us to do it when we got off the plane."

"Oh, God! Yes, I remember," said Izzie. "We were too busy watching Lucy chat up the Teddy bear."

We raced down the stairs, through the courtyard, and across the square to the café. We scoured the customers sitting at the tables. No sign of Mrs. Elwes. No sign of Mr. Johnson. No sign of any other girls in our class.

"Oh, pooh," said Izzie.

"What do we do now?" asked Nesta.

"Get a cab," I said. "We know the name of our hotel."

Nesta got her purse out and turned out the money in there. There were only a few notes left. "No way is this enough."

"Bus?" suggested T. J.

"There were a million at the station we passed. How would we know which one to get?" I asked.

"We could walk," said Nesta. "Does anyone remember the way back?"

Izzie, T. J., and I shook our heads.

Stranded on our first day in Florence. A fine start to our holiday, I thought as I looked around and tried not to panic.

Don't miss the next round of Truth or Dare!
Turn the page for an excerpt of . . .

starstruck

Cathy Hopkins

I AM A DEAD MAN, I thought. How will I ever be able to tell Mum and Dad?

I left the shop and went to look for Mac, who had taken off to another street to buy some oil pastels from an artist's supply shop. He wants to be a cartoonist when he leaves school. He can paint, draw, do illustrations, but really cartooning is his thing. He can capture anyone with just a few strokes of his pen. Takes talent, that does. You need an eye for the absolute essentials. It's a bit like photography; you have to have an eye for that too. It's one of the things we have in common as mates. We might go to the same college if we can find one that does film studies as well as cartooning and animation.

I crossed the road and as I went round the corner, I spotted Mac looking in the window of the art shop. He looked up and beckoned me over to him.

"Hey, come and look at this," he said, then he saw my face. "Not good news?"

I shook my head. "Think I'm going to need a small miracle this time. It'll cost a fortune to fix. Guy in the shop said I may as well get a new one, but no way can I afford one and I can't go to Cousin Ed or Jo to get it repaired, as word will get back to Dad."

"Maybe you should just bite the bullet and tell him," said Mac. "Accidents happen. He'll understand, won't he?"

"Yeah," I said. "And that's exactly way I don't want to tell him. Him being understanding would make it even worse. I know Mum and Dad really went out on a limb to get me that camcorder. I don't want to disappoint them. Let them down like a stupid kid who breaks his toy on Christmas morning. No, what I'll do is get a Saturday job. I'll work in the Easter holidays. I'll sort it."

Mac started grinning like an idiot.

"It's not funny, Mac."

"I know. I'm not smiling because of that. I'm smiling because someone up there must be looking after you."

"Yeah, right. And exactly where were they when I tripped over Rupert the Bear?"

"Look in the window," said Mac.

"What at?" I asked.

"At the notices," said Mac pointing to a notice-board on the left of the window. "One small miracle, I do believe."

There were loads of notices on postcards: flat to rent; bicycle for sale; cleaner needed.

"What?" I asked. "You suggesting I leave home and become a cleaner? I suppose I could sell my bike. Yeah. I guess that's an option. . . ."

Mac shook his head and pointed to a notice to the left of the others. "There, you dufus."

Then I saw it.

Ever wanted to work in the movies? Now is your chance.

Needed: extras, drivers, runners, cleaners, caterers.

Must be local.

Must be available between April 14 and May 5.

Want to know more? Call 07365 88921 and ask for Sandra.

The answer to my prayers, I thought. "That's in the Easter holidays," I gasped. "I wonder where exactly they're going to film."

I turned to Mac, but he was already on his mobile asking for someone named Sandra.